ABOUT JAMES

James Tedesco is a hugely popular NRL superstar who loves to help and motivate kids whenever and however he can.

James was born in the northern Sydney suburb of Ryde, New South Wales, and raised on a 100-hectare property in Menangle in Sydney's south-west, complete with its own football field with goalposts. He began playing rugby league when he was six and always dreamt of playing NRL.

Red vs Blue is his second book about 12-year-old Teddy. Like *Hat-Trick Teddy*, it is based on James's own footy-playing childho
and it encourages kids to follow th
regardless of the obstacle

JAMES TEDESCO

RED VS BLUE

PAN
Pan Macmillan Australia

Pan Macmillan acknowledges the Traditional Custodians of country throughout Australia and their connections to lands, waters and communities. We pay our respect to Elders past and present and extend that respect to all Aboriginal and Torres Strait Islander peoples today. We honour more than sixty thousand years of storytelling, art and culture.

First published 2021 in Sydney by Pan Macmillan Australia Pty Ltd
1 Market Street, Sydney, New South Wales, Australia, 2000

NATIONAL LIBRARY OF AUSTRALIA

A catalogue record for this book is available from the National Library of Australia

Typeset in LinoLetter by Billy Blue Creative

Printed by IVE

FSC www.fsc.org MIX Paper | Supporting responsible forestry FSC® C018183

The paper in this book is FSC® certified. FSC® promotes environmentally responsible, socially beneficial and economically viable management of the world's forests.

To the Camden Rams, my junior club where it all started. Thank you for igniting my dream and providing me with the opportunity to chase it.

My old rugby league club, the Menangle Meerkats, is no longer. Our playing fields turned into a mud-pit after a freak rainstorm and the carnival rides that were set up for the Menangle Show are still trapped in the ground there.

I was invited to play for the Camden Rams, but my best mates weren't. I made the team, and for a while it was hard not having my old friends to lean on. Luckily for me, Dad made a deal with the club president. If I broke the club scoring record against the Picton Magpies, they would create another Camden team that my dad would coach and my friends could be in.

My name is James Tedesco and I'm getting the old team back together again. I'm also one step closer to playing for my heroes, the Sydney Roosters. It's not just a dream anymore. I'm going to make it happen.

JAMES 'TEDDY' TEDESCO
-12 YEARS OLD

CHAPTER 1

VERY SERIOUS DAD

I look at Ben, Luke, Gerard and Alex, who are sprawled out, sweaty and exhausted, on the Camden Rams footy fields. The fact that Ben and I just versed Luke, Gerard and Alex and kicked their butts in a game of touch footy isn't the reason they're so tired.

The real reason is that before the game of footy today, we were chased by the trolley boys at Campbelltown Mall. It's a long story but I'll make it short: Luke asked out Breeanna Lee

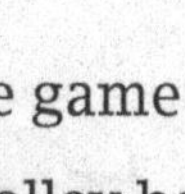

at her parents' cheese shop. (It specialises in goat's cheese – gross.) Breeanna is already going out with an older boy, Damir the trolley boy. Damir wasn't happy about Luke's romantic proposal and confronted us. Gerard teased one of the other trolley boys who has a try-hard beard, calling him 'Dog's Butt'. They ended up chasing us and we escaped by hiding in the basement of the mall.

When I get home that afternoon, I tell my family everything.

I tell them about Damir and his mates chasing us.

I tell them that the basement of the mall is kind of creepy but kind of cool.

I tell them that I never want to eat goat's cheese.

I tell them about how unfit the boys are.

Everyone in my family listens carefully as I describe what happened. They're all interested in different things.

Nonna likes hearing about Luke being in love.

Nonno keeps saying how much he likes the Lee family's cheese. *'Mi piace il formaggio!'* He really loves cheese.

Matthew doesn't stop laughing. 'That's a shame!' he says when I tell him about Luke asking Breeanna out.

Mum's worried. All she wants to know is if the police were involved.

Dad is **shocked** to hear how exhausted the boys were after our game. He's scribbling notes and ideas on the back of an old shopping list.

After I've finished the story, Dad stuffs the shopping list in the back pocket of his jeans. 'I've heard enough!' he exclaims. 'James, we've only got one chance to make this new team a success.'

Mum can see that Dad's getting worked up and maybe taking this a little too seriously.

'John, dear,' she says, but he waves her away.

'Sorry, love,' he replies. 'President Taber at the Camden Rams has created a new team and put me in charge. James sealed the deal for us last month and that's how the Camden Blue Under 12s was born,' he explains. 'And any team that John Tedesco coaches needs to be in shape.'

UH-OH!

GULP. I can see that he is serious.

Very serious.

Saturday nights are always movie night at the Tedesco house, but instead of eating dinner and watching *Mrs Doubtfire* with the family, Dad heads outside to the tractor shed. 'James?' he calls when he's halfway between the house and the shed. I run out to see him holding his dinner plate in one hand and a clipboard in the other. A ballpoint pen is resting behind his ear.

'Yeah, Dad?' I say.

'Tell everyone in the old Meerkats team that if they want to play footy again, they'll need to be here at 9.00 am tomorrow. After that we'll start our proper training on Tuesdays and Thursdays at the Rams' fields.'

He turns around, slides open the tractor shed door with his foot and turns on the light.

Before I message the old Meerkats team, I create a checklist based on our old starting line-up. If I can get them all to play again, we'll have a very competitive team. I'm excited.

But an hour or so later, after I've tracked everyone down with my invitation, this is how Camden Blue is looking:

CAMDEN RAMS BLUE

Captain: James Tedesco. Coach: John Tedesco

Position	Name	Playing?	Notes
Fullback	James Tedesco	✓	Might be running late. Kidding ☺
Wing	Thomas Mitchell	✗	Now plays soccer
Wing	Harry Holborn	✗	Moved to Gold Coast
Centre	Tawera Richard-son	✓	Sweet as, cuz
Wing	Milos Ristanovic	✗	Moved to Melbourne
Five-eighth	Charlie Day	✗	Moved house. Lives too far away.
Halfback	Gerard Quig	✓	Certain
Front Row	Hassan Ali	✗	Playing soccer with Thomas

Hooker	Ben Sarkis	✓	Certain
Front Row	Izaiah Tuaneti	✗	Gone to play rugby union. Meh.
Second Row	Luke Pollard	✓	Certain
Second Row	Ryan Gallagher	✗	Broken arm (skateboard)
Lock	Patty Daly	✓	Certain (after he does his hair and shines his boots)
Inter-change	Dexter Collins	✓	Dexie baby is back, baby
Inter-change	Jack Patch	✗	Moved to Lismore
Inter-change	Lazlo Pere	✗	Still in New Zealand
Inter-change	Tobias Paulo	✓	Certain

By the time I've finished the list, I crunch the numbers and realise that we only have a run-on squad of eight players. We're five players short, not counting reserves. Alex's mum won't let him play and Lewis isn't that sporty, so those two are off the cards. Still, eight players in a team is better than no team at all.

The laughter coming from the lounge room has stopped, which means that either the movie has finished or everyone has fallen asleep. Nonno's favourite part in the movie is when Mrs Doubtfire's bra catches fire on the stove, and tonight I heard him laughing so much he coughed up a meatball. Nonna got cranky at him for not chewing his food properly. When I walk out to the lounge room, the only person there is Matthew, watching the late-night NBA game from America.

'You got a team yet?' he asks, not taking his eyes off the TV. LeBron James from the

Los Angeles Lakers drives past the Detroit Pistons' guards and slam dunks the ball through the hoop. The crowd goes wild.

'Can you turn that TV down, Matthew?' yells Mum from her bedroom. Matthew points the remote at the TV like a lightsabre and quickly adjusts the volume.

'Eight players coming back, and we'll need to find a heap of new players,' I say.

'Big job. Good luck, little bro,' says Matthew, still glued to the Lakers game. I peer out the window to the dark of the yard and see that the light is still on in the tractor shed.

There's already a thick dew on the grass as I walk barefoot across the paddock to the shed. I shine the torch carefully in front of me to dodge the cow poo. When I reach the doorway, Dad is putting the finishing touches on tomorrow's training session on the big shiny whiteboard that rests on top of his workbench. How can I tell him that we don't even have a full team? He notices me at the door. 'What do you think?' he asks, looking proudly at his work.

'Um, it's great,' I say. He gives me that look. It's the same look he gives me when he knows I'm not telling him something.

1. Like the time I hit a cricket ball and accidentally smashed the head off Dad's favourite garden statue and I was too scared to confess.

2. Like the time I accidentally left the fish from the market in Dad's ute and he was wondering what the smell was a week later.

3. Like the time I tried to prank Matthew by putting cling wrap across the toilet but I got Dad instead.

NUMBER 2S!

'What's wrong, James?' he asks, putting the lid on his whiteboard marker. 'This is supposed to be exciting.'

I fidget nervously with my fingers before coming out with it.

'Me, Luke, Ben, Gerard, Tawera, Patty, Dexter and Tobias are the only definites,' I tell him.

Dad looks puzzled.

'Milos?' he asks.

'Melbourne,' I say.

'Hassan?'

'Soccer,' I say.

'Thomas?' he asks.

'Same as Hassan.' I show Dad the whole list, but in typical Tedesco style, nothing is going to beat him.

'Oh well, let's work with what we've got,' he says cheerfully. 'We'll find some new players later. But for now, it's bedtime.' He yawns. As Dad lifts the whiteboard off the workbench and onto the tractor trailer

ready for tomorrow, I catch a glimpse of what awaits us in the morning.

Something tells me that I need to get some sleep too.

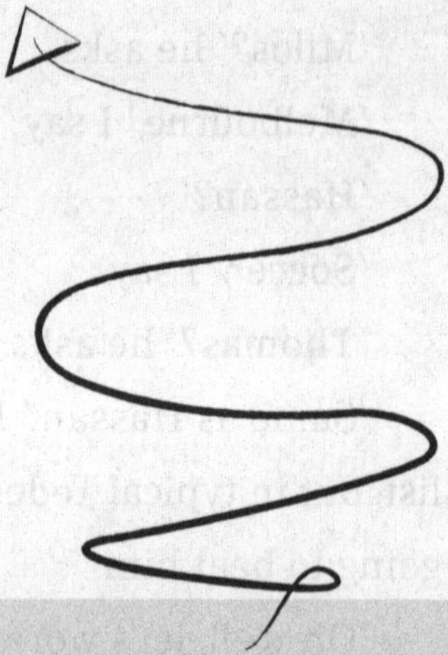

Teddy's Tips No. 1

Better out than in!

Don't bottle things up. Speak to those around you. Help is just a conversation away.

CHAPTER 2

THE GOAT WHISPERER

Dad's been up since before sunrise mowing the field and repainting the sidelines. His whiteboard stands proudly on the back of the trailer in the middle of the paddock. Matt and I have helped him get the witches' hats, balls and equipment ready.

Soon, there's a steady line of cars coming up the farm's long, winding driveway. Parents drop their boys at the top of the paddock, wave at Dad and thank him for giving their sons the chance to play footy again.

'It's nothing, really,' Dad says humbly through their car windows. But deep down, I know he has the same dream that I have – to beat Coach Sharpe and those show-offs in Camden Red.

As I watch the boys arrive in their training gear, I realise that the last time we all played together was last season for the Menangle Meerkats. Like a well-oiled machine, the eight of us come to the middle of the field and begin our stretches. Dad launches into his welcome speech. 'Good morning, boys, and welcome to the Camden Rams Blue team,' he announces.

'Good mor-ning, Mis-ter Te-des-co,' the boys say in unison, like they're saying good morning to their teacher at school.

'This isn't class, this is training!' says Dad, pacing around us. He's wearing his black rubber knee-high gumboots and red Nike tracksuit. It has COACH printed across the back of the jacket in large white letters. 'No more Mr Tedesco, you can call me Coach,' he instructs.

'Do you reckon we can win the grand final, Coach?' asks Ben. Dad stops pacing and considers Ben's question.

'Let's not get ahead of ourselves,' Dad says seriously. 'From what I've heard, you fellas need to work on your fitness first.'

Ben, Luke and Gerard look at me

ACCUSINGLY

as they realise I must have told Dad how puffed they were after the chase through the mall and our touch footy game yesterday.

'That's true,' says Tobias. 'Mum just got us a pie maker and that's all I've been eating.' Everyone looks at Tobias. He's definitely not in good shape. 'Meat pies, apple pies, cherry pies, chicken pies, chicken and curry pies, steak pies, steak and mushroom pies –'

'Okay, time to finish up your stretches now,' says Dad, trying to refocus us.

'– beef pies, beef and bacon pies, mushy pea pies –' continues Tobias.

'Enough about pies!'

shouts Dad. Tobias stops. Dad looks around at the group.

'Two laps around the field – no stopping!' he says, catching us off guard. 'Anyone who stops will earn the team 20 burpees!' Everyone looks straight at Tobias.

'What?' says Tobias, shrugging.

I lead by example and start the run. 'Keep a steady pace!' I tell the team. 'This is just a warm-up!' We all complete one lap, but just like yesterday, I can already hear the panting behind me. When I turn around, everyone is red in the face and Tobias has slowed to a shuffle. 'Come on, guys, we can do this!' I yell. Gerard has a gritty look of determination on his face. I know he'll finish this second lap without stopping. Dexter gives me a silent nod.

He'll push through as well.

Half a lap to go. Dad has one leg up on the trailer and is watching us carefully and taking notes on his clipboard. Tobias is gasping for air.

'Come on, Tobias, you can do it!' I yell down the field.

'No . . . no. I . . . can't,' he gasps, his knees about to buckle from exhaustion. If he stops we'll have a penalty of

20 BURPEES.

Patty, our lock, is right near him.

'Noooooooo!' screams Patty, almost in slow motion. Patty runs over and catches

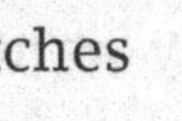

Tobias by the arm, throwing it around his shoulders. 'Keep jogging, mate, you've got this,' he encourages Tobias.

Tobias, sweating, puffing and nearly dead, leans heavily on Patty and puts one foot in front of the other. The rest of us cheer them on. Finally, they cross the finish line.

'Great determination,' Dad says, running over and patting Tobias and Patty on the back. 'Great teamwork as well.' But everyone is concentrating on gulping down water from their drink bottles.

After a couple of minutes' rest, Dad moves on to the next part of the training session. He tells us to get into pairs and gather around the whiteboard. We listen carefully and study his scribbling and diagrams.

'This is a fitness circuit,' he explains. 'You and your partner have two minutes at each station and will do four laps of the circuit.'

Everyone squabbles about which station they want to start on. Ben and I shotgun the tractor tyre throw. Luke and Gerard bags the shuttle runs. Tawera and Patty start with sit-ups and Dexter and Tobias begin with the boxing pads. Dad tells us to get ready. We all race to our stations and begin when we hear the music coming from the speakers on the back of the trailer. It's Dad's favourite band – AC/DC.

After the first two circuits, I notice Dad standing in the middle of his players, proudly watching on as we sweat through his gruelling training session. He taps his foot to the chorus of 'Thunderstruck'. Suddenly, the smile on his face is replaced by a look of horror.

'No! No! No!' he yells, looking off into the distance. 'Not my roses!' We all follow his gaze to the side of the field where Dad has his prize-winning rose garden. Munching happily on the soft pink petals of Dad's blooming flowers is a goat. Not just any goat, but a big daddy billygoat. The bushes have been chewed to pieces and now he's finishing off the last few flowers.

I **DROP** the tyre.

Gerard **STOPS** shuttling.

Tawera **FREEZES** halfway through a sit-up.

Dexter accidentally **PUNCHES** Tobias in the face.

'Get him out of there!' screams Dad. He's the coach, so that's exactly what we try to do. We run like a pack of lunatics towards the rose garden. Old man billygoat looks up in fright and sees eight charging 12-year-olds running towards him.

'Corner him!' I say, jumping Dad's wire fence. Any fatigue from the training session has been replaced by pure adrenaline. The goat looks at us and it's clear he feels threatened by these sweaty boys interrupting his Sunday brunch.

'Baaaaaa,' he bleats. As he backs up into the corner of the garden, his red collar rattles around his neck. There's a shiny gold tag that says 'Easy Cheesy Farm' hanging from it.

'He's come over from Breeanna's house, Dad,' I say.

'Well, they can replace my roses,' Dad scowls. The goat is still staring deep into my soul.

'That's a good boy, we're not going to hurt you,' I say, glancing at his massive pointy horns. The goat stomps his feet. He looks like he's ready to attack us at any second. Luke comes up next to me.

'He's scared. You're doing this all wrong, Teddy,' he whispers.

'What would you do, then?' I ask, still watching the goat's every move. Luke does a lot of weird stuff, but today he wins the grand final of weird.

'This,' he says. 'Stand back, everyone.'

We all move back a few steps but Luke steps forward and starts singing.

'Breeeee-annnna!
Breeeee-annnna!
Eyes like the moon,
Smile like a ray of sunshiiiine.'

Immediately the goat relaxes. He stops stomping and bleating and looks calmly at Luke. Soon enough, he trots over and rubs his head against Luke's leg like a puppy dog.

'Whoa!' we all say.

'Where did you learn that, bro?' asks Tawera.

'Don't know,' Luke replies. 'It's a gift.'

Meanwhile, Dad has been on the phone

to Mr Lee. He and Breeanna speed up the driveway in their ute and come to a screeching halt next to the garden.

'Take it easy on them, Dad,' I say quietly. He makes a 'lips-zipped' motion with his hand, crosses his arms and rocks from side to side.

'Sorry about this, John,' says Mr Lee. 'I don't know how Rocco escaped.'

Breeanna comes up and ruffles the hair between Rocco's horns.

'He's always naughty around strangers. How did you get him to behave, Luke?' she asks.

'It's a gift, he reckons,' says Tawera.

'Well, thank you, Luke.' Breeanna smiles, then she gives Luke a hug. He blushes. Lucky there are no trolley boys around.

Mr Lee and Breeanna walk Rocco over to their ute and put him in the back. Just before they drive away, I remember the sign on display in their shop, Easy Cheesy.

'How do you make cheese from Rocco?'

I yell. Breeanna laughs at me.

'We make the cheese from the females' milk. The boys don't make milk.' She shakes her head as if this is the silliest thing she's ever heard.

'Oh,' I say, embarrassed.

'What about pies?' yells Tobias. 'Do you make goat pie? Goat and potato pie? Creamy goat and onion pie?'

But Breanna and her dad are already halfway down the driveway in a cloud of dust.

Teddy's Tips No. 2

The warm-up

Warming up before you train or play is super important to prevent injuries and to ensure you perform at your peak. I always stretch all body parts from the top down.

CHAPTER 3

YEAH THE BOYS

My eyes open to see the sun shining through my bedroom window and reflecting off my Sydney Roosters alarm clock. Today is a special day. It's the first time we officially play as Camden Blue. After eating seven Weet-Bix and drinking a cold glass of Milo, I start my pre-game ritual of putting my headphones on and listening to music. Today I've chosen my favourite rapper, MC Lil-Earl. As we drive to the game in

Mum's car, which still has the JAMES TEDESCO – SPONSORED BY JULIE'S HAIR AND BEAUTY sticker plastered over it, I visualise the plays we've been practising as a team. While our fitness is still improving, we haven't forgotten any of our skills.

We're playing the Moss Vale Dragons. We haven't had time to recruit extra players, so Dad has already called their coach and asked if we can borrow some of their reserves to make a full team. Unlike Coach Sharpe from Camden Red, the Moss Vale coach is very kind and agrees to lend us five players, which gives us a full team with no reserves.

It's five minutes before kick-off and we are getting ready in the visitors' dressing shed. The sight of the boys in new colours takes a bit of getting used to. We've gone from the yellow and blue of the Meerkats to the red, white and blue of the Rams. Now I'm not the only Meerkat who's turned into a Ram.

'Tawera, you good to go at centre?' asks Dad. Tawera is in the zone. He gives Dad a serious nod and goes back to taping his boots. 'Patty, I need you moving fast – keep the Dragons on their toes.'

'No problem, Coach,' he replies, putting product in his hair and checking himself out in the mirror.

'To our players from the Dragons, thanks for helping out,' says Dad. It's a bit weird having players from another club in our team, but with only eight team members, we'll take what we can get. They mumble something about not having a choice and look about as excited as ice cubes on a rocket to the sun.

The boys and I line up near the door of the shed, our plastic studs click-clacking on the tiles, ready to run out. We've all got our mouthguards in and we're dead quiet, concentrating on Dad's individual instructions earlier on. Patty's still at the mirror.

'One more thing,' says Dad from the back of the shed, his voice echoing off the walls. We all turn to face him. 'Remember to have fun.' He smiles. 'You've got this.'

The referee blows his whistle and we run to the centre of the field and shake hands with the opposition players. The Dragons players on loan to us laugh as they shake their usual teammates' hands. This might be funny to them, but the rest of us are taking this game very seriously. When the referee flips the coin, I call heads and win the toss. Dragons will kick to us.

'You ready?' I say to my team as we all take position.

'Let's do this!' yells Gerard.

'YEAH THE BOYS,'

screams Ben.

The ball is sent deep downfield from the kick-off and falls into the hands of Dexter at wing. He runs it up bravely, the first time in months that he's had the opposition closing in on him. He looks to pass it.

'Hold it!' I tell him, and he does.

Two Dragons players tackle him but he loses the ball as he falls to the ground. Another Dragons player, close behind, scoops up the loose ball and runs unmarked all the way to the tryline and scores.

'Don't worry, mate,' I say to Dexter, running over to him. Dexter has his head down. He's obviously disappointed with his mistake.

'Sorry, boys,' he says, but the others have their heads down as well. This isn't the start any of us wanted. The Dragons' kicker misses the conversion and after two minutes, we're already trailing 4–0. As we walk back to kick off to them, I pull Gerard, our kicker, over to the side.

'We need to lift the team,' I say. 'Let's put on a bit of a show – you and me.'

'Short ball?' He smiles. 'Like the good old days?' He makes it sound like we're a couple of grandpas.

'Short ball.' I smile back through my mouthguard. 'Good old days.'

Gerard gives me a wink and takes five steps backwards, indicating that this will be a long kick, but I know better. As he runs towards the ball, he slows his last two steps and kicks the ball short instead. The Dragons players up front are caught off guard as I chase the ball and watch it carefully sail towards the 40-metre line. When the ball starts to fall and is within reach, I launch myself into the air and catch it on the full. Instantaneously, my Spidey senses kick in and I can see the game of join-the-dots play out in my head. It's time to do my thing.

- Step left and draw in their second rower / Step right.

Dot joined.

- Keep running and dummy to Patty on the left / Pass to Gerard supporting on the right instead.

Dot joined.

- Call for the ball and wrap Gerard / Catch it safely and draw in their centre.

Dot joined.

- Make sure Gerard is running at the gap their centre has created / Fire the ball back to Gerard.

Dot joined.

- Gerard veers left from the defenders coming across from the right / He scores under the post.

Mission accomplished!

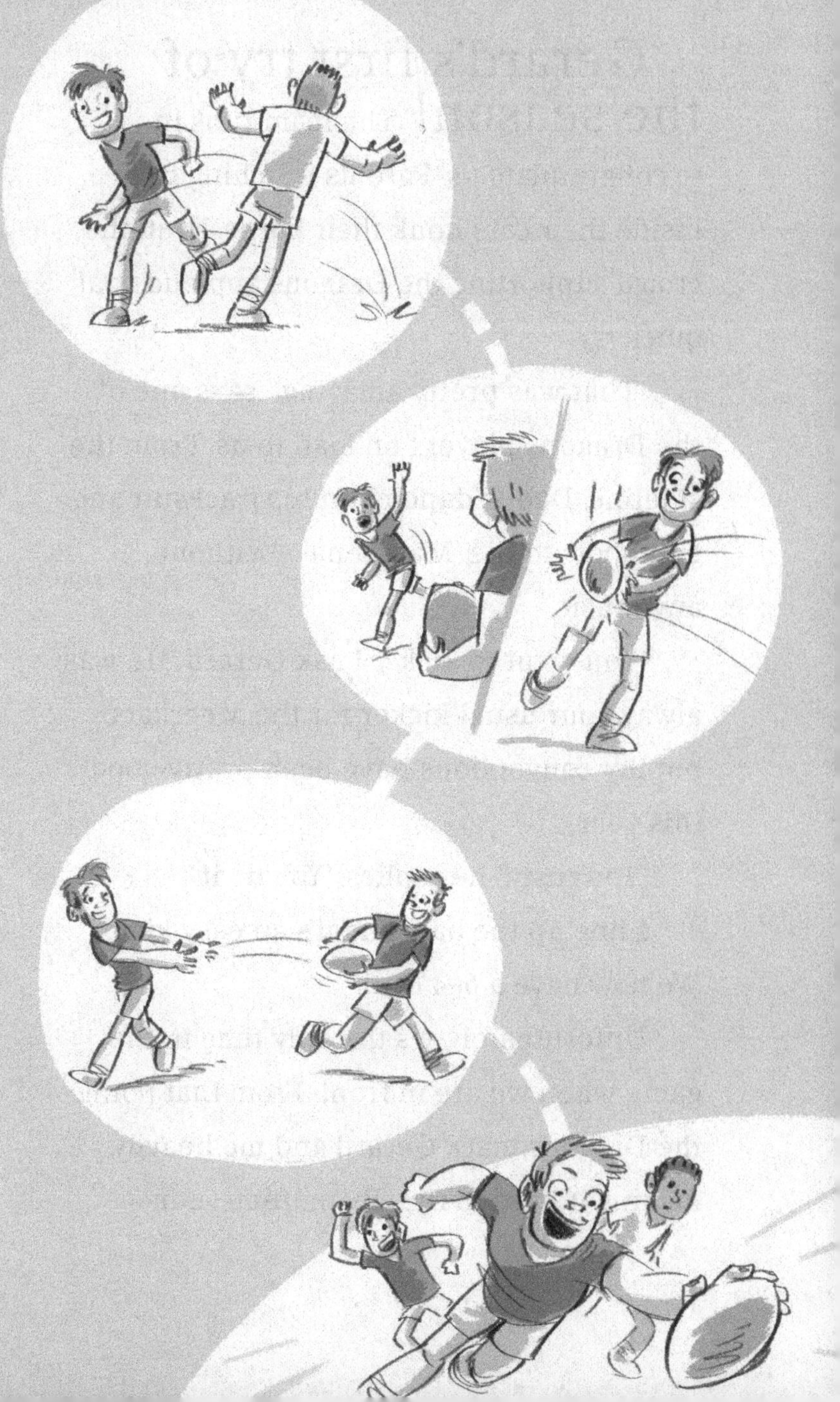

Gerard's first try of the season! The team runs in to congratulate us. Parents watching from inside their cars honk their horns. Even the crowd supporting the Dragons applauds our quick try.

'That was pretty amazing,' says one of the Dragons players on loan to us. From the sideline, Dad is dancing in his tracksuit and gumboots to the 'Macarena' – without any music.

'You want to kick?' I ask Gerard. He was always our usual kicker for the Meerkats, but my conversions have been pretty good this year.

'Too rusty,' he replies. 'You do it.'

I line up the ball, and it's an easy kick. We now have a 6–4 lead.

Unfortunately, it's the only time in the game when we are in front. From that point, the Dragons mark Gerard and me heavily, making it hard to run. By halftime, our players are dead on their feet, but they push through bravely. In the end, our defence has more holes in it than a box of cinnamon donuts. We are flogged 58 points to six.

'Don't worry about it, boys,' says Dad as we walk from the field. 'It was always going to be hard starting later in the season.'

I know Dad is just trying to be encouraging but I hate getting our butt kicked.

'They beat us by 52 points, Dad!' I say, exasperated. 'It was a cricket score!'

Dad doesn't answer. Instead, he stands quietly next to the washing basket he's brought from home to collect the dirty jerseys in.

'Sorry, Coach. Sorry, Teddy,' mumble some of the boys as they walk past dejectedly, each tossing their shirt on the pile. The excitement of starting a new season with the Rams has already rubbed off after our huge loss.

'Once we improve our fitness, the rest will fall into place,' Dad says to me in his soft voice. This usually comes out when he's been thinking seriously about something.

'There's something else our team needs,' I say.

'What is it?' he asks.

'Players,' I say. 'We need to go on a player hunt.'

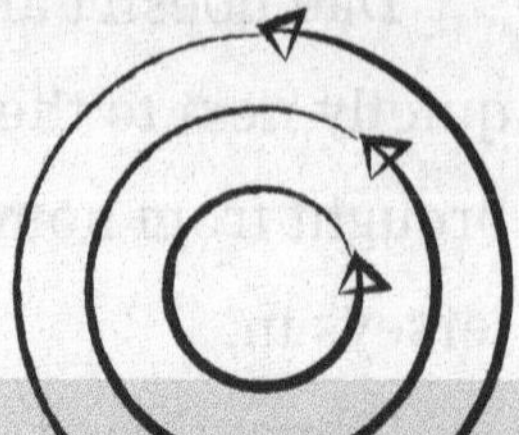

Teddy's Tips No. 3

Kick-offs

Pick your kicking target. Keep your head down and kick through the ball. Don't rush. Have a signal for the other players in your team to make sure they stay onside.

CHAPTER 4

DO YOU  EVEN HAVE PANTS ON?

There's a rule in our house after school – business before pleasure. That means homework and chores need to be finished before we can watch TV, play on devices, go outside or go to footy training.

This afternoon is no different. I smash through my Maths and then put the finishing touches on my Design and Technology assignment. Lewis and I have teamed up to create a new stud design for a pair of footy boots.

I've just finished the sketches on my iPad so I can show Lewis tomorrow. If our design is good enough, Miss Warren will let us enter it into the 3D design software and print it on the 3D printer.

As I'm closing down the sketch app and opening up another program, I allow myself to daydream and pretend that Nike will love the design so much, they'll decide to start making our boots.

All the superstars in the NRL will be wearing them and will tell everyone during the fulltime interviews how fast they make them run. Nike will give Lewis and me unlimited shoes for life and –

'Is there a reason you have Skype open?' asks Mum, walking into my bedroom. Her voice startles me.

'Yes, Mum, the boys are about to log on.'

'Which boys?'

'Camden Blue,' I explain. 'We're coming up with a plan to recruit more players. Don't worry, I've finished my homework.'

Mum smiles, ruffles my hair, freshly cut by Julie's Hair and Beauty. 'You and your footy,' she says, smiling. 'You must have been born with a football in your hands.'

I think about that for a minute and realise she's joking. That would be kind of weird – a crying and slimy baby with a footy under its arm.

A ringing noise comes from the iPad. A little Skype window opens and Gerard appears. 'Teddy!' he says. His voice is echoing like he's in a hallway or something.

'Where are you?' I say. All I can see behind him is white and a spray can of something. It's certainly not his bedroom. If it was, the wall would be covered in BMX posters.

'I'm in the bathroom,' he says. 'The wi-fi is good in here.'

Now I realise he must be sitting on the toilet. **'Dude! Gross!'** I say. 'Do you even have pants on?' But before he can answer, Ben logs on. Then Dexter. Then Tobias. Then Luke. After a couple of minutes, all eight members of Camden Blue are on the Skype call.

'Thanks for coming to the meeting, fellas,' I say. They all go to say something but I can't understand them. It sounds like a swarm of bees when everyone talks at once.

'Put yourselves on mute, please,' I say. 'When it's your turn to talk, then you can unmute.' A little message pops up on my screen from Ben.

Bossy boots

it says.

'You're all here because we need more players. Our old Meerkats crew aren't coming back, so we need some new blood.'

Tobias signals that he wants to speak. He unmutes himself.

'Don't we need players? Why would we need blood?' he asks.

'We don't really need blood – it's just a figure of speech,' I say.

'A what?' says Tobias.

I decide to mute him myself.

'Guys, we need ideas,' I tell them.

'Where can we get some new players?'

I scan the screen and I can see that everyone is deep in thought. Some are scratching their heads, some are looking down at the ground, searching for answers. Finally, Luke unmutes himself.

'We need to visit places where people have the skills we're looking for,' he says.

'Like where?' I ask.

'Well, if we want fast players, we should go to the Little Athletics track on Friday night and see who's running,' he says. 'Whoever wins the sprints is the person we want.'

'Yes! Great idea, Luke,' I say. 'Any other ideas?' I ask.

'Some tall players would be good,' says Ben. 'We could visit the basketball courts too.'

'Let's do that!' I say excitedly. I'm surprised at all the good ideas so far. The boys are getting excited as well.

'We need some front rowers,' says Tawera. 'Really big ones!' he adds.

'Will you find them at the gym?' I ask.

'Nah – at KFC!' he says. Everyone cracks up. But then we see from the look on his face that Tawera's not joking.

Once they've given me their ideas, we decide to divide the team into pairs and do a recruitment drive on the weekend. We have a bye this round, so there's no game of footy anyway. The roster looks like this:

Teddy and Luke:
Camden Little Athletics
Ben and Gerard:
Camden Valley Basketball Club
Tawera and Dexter:
KFC Campbelltown
Patty and Tobias:
Narellan Vale Touch Football Club

Dexter has offered to pick up a bundle of registration forms from the Camden Rams Rugby League Club. Tobias is writing a script for us to speak from. He's going to email it out tomorrow. It's important that we're all saying the same thing, he reckons. I'm going to ask Julie's Hair and Beauty for some sample bags to hand out. It's better than nothing.

The Skype meeting is nearly finished. Everyone knows their jobs and what type of players they're looking for. The goal is to have a full run-on team by the following weekend.

'Good luck, everyone,' I say before we log off for the night. 'Hopefully we'll have some new players at training next Tuesday.'

From out of nowhere, everyone erupts in laughter.

I look at them in confusion. What did I say? Bringing new players to training isn't *that* funny. In fact, it's not funny at all. So why is Gerard laughing his head off, bouncing up and down on the toilet?

That's when I realise they're not laughing at me – they're cracking up at something in the background of my screen. I spin around and see my brother Matt wearing his big red headphones and a bath towel around his waist. He's fresh out of the shower, dancing and singing into Mum's hairbrush. He has no idea that I'm on a Skype call. He thinks he's Justin Bieber singing to the girls. Some of the team mute themselves because they're laughing so hard. Matt continues to shake his butt and thrust his hips down the hallway, totally unaware of the audience watching his cool moves. Suddenly, the sound of laughter is cut short by a loud

CLUNK.

Gerard has dropped his device, and for a split second, his window turns black before the bathroom reappears with the camera pointed up at the ceiling. And that's when we see it. My question about whether Gerard has any pants on is answered.

Teddy's Tips No. 4

Stay positive

You will always face obstacles. Challenging situations are opportunities to grow. Stay positive and calm and you'll be okay.

CHAPTER 5

BOOTS AND ALL

The gang at school are buzzing.

Last night's Skype call boosted everyone's mood. The Camden Blue players who go to St Gregory's are all talking about this week's recruitment drive. The players who go to other schools are messaging us back and forth. Luke answers a text message from Tobias, puts his phone away and walks over to where I'm having lunch.

'Teddy, I don't want to sound like I'm

sucking up, but you were a good leader yesterday. Just look at how pumped we are,' he says, pointing at the crew.

'Thanks.' I smile, putting down the half-eaten slice of cold leftover pizza that Nonno made for dinner last night. It's covered in ham, cheese, olives and his top-secret pizza sauce. 'But remember, we're all leaders,' I say. 'Doing what's right for our team is leadership.'

'Yeah, I guess you're right.' Luke smiles back, stuffing half a sausage and tomato sauce sandwich into his mouth. It looks pretty good, too. 'I just hope that we can attract some gun players – I want to beat those big-noters from Camden Red.' Little bits of bread and sausage spray out of his mouth like machine-gun bullets as he chews and speaks at the same time.

'Me too,' I say. 'That would be the best.'

The bell rings for the last session of the day. It's the moment I've been waiting for all week. Lewis and I will finally find out if Miss Warren has chosen our Design and Technology assignment as the best in the class. If she has, we get to print our footy boots stud design on the 3D printer. As class goes in, we all sit with our project partners and watch Miss Warren hook up her laptop to display the rough sketches on the smartboard.

'Congratulations, boys,' she says to the class. 'I was very impressed with your original and innovative ideas.' Miss Warren is always very bright and encouraging. She can find the positive in anything.

'We've got this, bro,' whispers Lewis, leaning in and fist-bumping me. Lewis is big. His hands are twice the size of mine. He's also the St Gregory's Year 7 Maths and Science champion. I just wish he was allowed to play footy. I want to be as confident as Lewis, but as Miss Warren beams the designs up on the board, I'm not so sure ours will be her favourite.

'Steven? Marley? I absolutely love this

design. What did you say it was again?' she asks Steven and Marley, who are sitting up the back.

'We call it a **poo claw,** Miss,' says Steven. 'You put the dog poo bag on the plastic claw and then scoop up the poo. Your hands won't even need to feel the warm poo through the plastic bag.' The class giggles, but it's actually a good idea. Miss Warren nods appreciatively and clicks over to the next one.

'Harrison and Bodie, this looks rather familiar. Can you explain how it works?' This time the class turns to the front where Harrison and Bodie are sitting.

'We call it a coathanger, Miss,' replies Bodie. 'You can put a shirt on it and hang it in your wardrobe.'

Bodie turns and high-fives his partner, Harrison. They seem to be really happy with their design, even though it's not the most original thing we've seen.

'Indeed,' says Miss Warren, raising her

eyebrows. 'And can you explain how it's different from a normal coathanger?'

'Good question, Miss,' says Harrison. 'The big difference is that ours is red, so it goes faster.'

Miss Warren rolls her eyes, but she's smiling. Then she moves on to the exciting part.

'Well, I hope you're all ready for our winner,' she announces. 'I have the design software ready for these two boys and I'll even let them take the 3D printer home.'

The class murmurs excitedly – no has ever been allowed to take the printer home!

Once the class settles, Miss Warren displays the winning design. 'Congratulations Lewis Leota and James Tedesco for your new football boot stud design!'

'Whoa!' says the class at once. Their mouths are open. They haven't seen anything like this before. Lewis smiles proudly and puts an arm around me. He squeezes so hard I'm nearly suffocating.

'What's the name of your design?' says Miss Warren. The class is silent, waiting for an answer. Lewis clears his throat.

'We call it the Stealth Stud,' he says matter-of-factly. Then he gets out of his chair and walks towards the smartboard. He points at the stud pattern and continues. 'Teddy and I wanted to design studs for a footy boot that maximise speed and agility.' The class whispers excitedly to each other. 'The arrow-shaped blades are short enough to allow the boot to grip the grass, but won't let the player slip over. Because the blades are shorter, it takes less time to control your step, meaning you can run faster and glide over the grass.' Miss Warren is at the side of the classroom with her hands clasped together, smiling and bouncing from side to side.

'Teddy, do you want to explain the blades on the side of the sole?' asks Lewis. He motions me to join him at the front. We look like two scientists lecturing university students.

'The side blades are even shorter than the arrow blades,' I say. 'They let the player step left or right much faster than any other boot that's been made.' By now, everyone is out of their chair, commenting and asking questions, and one kid even asks if he can put in an order for a pair of Stealth Studs. Luckily, we're saved by the bell and it's home time.

'What am I going to do with this?' says Lewis as he walks towards the front gate. He's carrying the 3D printer on his shoulder and has a coil of plastic 3D printing filament in his hand.

'Take it home,' I say. 'Once we've put the design into the software, we can print out our first pair of studs.' Lewis sits down on the bench at the bus stop. Every day he catches the 887 bus home to Campbelltown.

'I can't,' he says sadly. 'My mother and father won't approve. They'll say I'm time-wasting.' He looks down at his shiny black school shoes and scuffs them in the dust.

'They expect me to concentrate on my maths and science. Can we keep it at your place?'

I see Mum's car in the distance. It's easy to spot with the Julie's Hair and Beauty sticker plastered on the side. I think Lewis's question through quickly.

'There's no room at my place,' I say, which is true. If we're going to pump out a heap of Stealth Studs, we're going to need a dedicated workspace that isn't filled up with my dad's farming equipment.

We need somewhere

SECRET.

Somewhere safe. That's when an idea hits me.

'Hi, James!' says Mum, pulling up at the bus stop. Nonna is in the front passenger seat.

'Ciao, ragazzi!' says Nonna, smiling with her bright-red lipstick.

'Hi, Mum, hi, Nonna,' I say. 'Hey, can we give Lewis a lift home?'

'Sure,' says Mum.

'And can we stop at the mall first?' I ask.

'What's going on?' whispers Lewis.

'Just follow my lead. I know where to put the printer,' I whisper back. We put our bags and the printer carefully in the boot while Mum and Nonna wave at Matt as he walks towards the car.

'I hope you know what you're doing,' Lewis says to me. Matt climbs in and closes the door behind him. Mum puts the car in gear and drives towards the mall.

'So do I,' I say.

Teddy's Tips No. 5

Teamwork

Communicate loudly and clearly with your teammates and work together in attack and defence. It's a team sport and there's no 'I' in team!

CHAPTER 6

MICHAEL WITH AN 'M'

The athletics track and the footy field are very similar, especially on a Friday night.

The field lights, towering over the track and grandstand, are shining brightly and the crowd is slowly building. Parents, grandparents, uncles and aunties are all starting to fill the stands to watch their family members compete. Just like our rugby league games, there is a canteen at the bottom of the grandstand that fills the air

with the amazing smell of hot chips, burgers and a sausage sizzle.

But tonight, we're not here for the food or the atmosphere. We're at the athletics track to recruit players for Camden Blue. Operation Track Attack!

'Got the stuff ready?' I say to Luke, but there's no need for him to answer. He points at the Julie's Hair and Beauty sample bags and Camden Rams Rugby League registration forms sitting at his feet on the cold concrete floor. Luke and I have memorised the script that Tobias has written. This is how it goes:

> *Hi, our names are* [insert your name here]. *What's yours?* [wait for them to answer] *You're really impressive. Ever thought about playing rugby league?* [wait for them to say yes] *You would be a great asset to the Camden Rams Blue team.*

We train on Tuesday and Thursday nights and play on Friday nights and some Saturday mornings.

Would you like to join us?

[wait for them to say yes]

**Remember to shake their hand and smile a lot.*

All the events for the little kids are first. Tonight's program says the Under 12s are on at 6.30 pm.

Luke and I scan the crowd, looking for boys our age who are already in their running gear. We see some down the front, stretching and warming up. One boy with brown hair with a track down the side and wearing a club singlet with light blue and dark blue stripes is sipping on a water bottle and listening to his headphones. His pre-race routine reminds me of mine. Focused, chilled and determined. He looks like a lean, mean running machine. I can already tell that he's the person I want. Soon enough, he takes his headphones off and walks up to the starting line. 'Ladies and gentlemen, the Under 12 boys 200-metre sprint is about to start,' says the voice over the loudspeakers.

'Go, Michael!' yells someone in our stand. 'Go, Michael, you're deadly!' yells someone else. It looks like his mum. The racers get set, they crouch down low – and

BANG!

They're off and running. I watch Michael break out of the blocks, his legs a blur as he and two other boys move to the front. The next runners are at least ten metres behind them and the gap is widening. There are shrieks and yelling coming from the grandstand – everyone is glued to the race. Michael and another boy move ahead of the third runner. It's going to be a close finish. They reach the 100-metre mark; they are halfway there.

'Michael Malone and Jared Little from the Camden Athletics Club lead the way. This will go down to the wire, folks,' says the announcer. The shrieking and yelling from the crowd starts back up. The runners are neck and neck. 'Fifty metres!' booms the announcer into the microphone. Luke and I are on our feet, watching Michael push in front – only just. As they cross the line, Michael heaves his chest forward, winning by less than half a metre. A huge cheer comes from around the track. Everyone shows their appreciation for such a closely run race.

'He's our man, quick, let's go!' I say to Luke. As we walk down the stairs of the grandstand holding a sample bag and going over the lines of the script in our heads, the scoreboard in the middle of the field lights up.

It says:

Under 12 Boys
200 metres

1st
M Malone
25.51 seconds

2nd
J Little
25.80 seconds

3rd
J Savage
27.13 seconds

Michael is at the finish line with his hands on his knees. Then he stands up straight and shakes hands with the other runners. Good sportsmanship – I like him already.

Before I can introduce myself, Luke takes a deep breath, plasters a smile on his face (like Tobias told us to) and slides himself between Michael and another runner.

'Hi, our names are . . . ' Then he stops and looks blank. He's practised the script so much without actually saying our names, he forgets what comes next.

'Luke and Teddy,' I whisper.

'Luke and Teddy,' he says, then suddenly remembers to smile again. He looks petrified, in a friendly way. Michael looks at Luke, then at me. I can tell he's a bit weirded out.

'What's yours?' asks Luke, sounding like a robot.

'What's my what?' says Michael with a puzzled look on his face.

'Your name,' answers Luke.

'Oh, it's Michael,' he says. 'With an "M".'

Luke looks really confused at Michael's joke but then suddenly remembers to smile again.

'You're really impressive,' continues Robot Luke. 'Ever thought about playing rugby league?' Then he says, 'Wait for them to say yes.'

'You're not supposed to say that part,' I whisper. 'You're just supposed to think it!'

Michael's eyes are like dinner plates. He must think we have concussion.

'You would be a great asset to the Camden Rams Blue team,' Luke continues. 'We train on Tuesday and Thursday nights and play on Friday nights and some Saturday mornings.' Luke's nearly finished saying the script. Only a few more words until we can ask Michael to be a Camden Ram. 'Would you like to join us?' Luke asks, but I can tell he's not finished. *Don't say it, don't say it, don't say it,* I think to myself.

But he does. He actually does. 'Wait for them to say yes,' finishes Luke.

'Wait for who?' asks Michael. At this point, I make a captain's call and decide to take over. I should have stepped in four lines ago.

'What Luke meant to say is, you've got amazing speed. Would you consider playing rugby league for the Under 12s Camden Rams Blue team?'

In the background, another cheer goes up. The announcer is getting the crowd ready for the next race.

'Hmm, maybe,' answers Michael. 'But only if I can bring someone with me,' he adds.

'Who?' I ask.

'Her,' he says, pointing back towards the track. A girl crouches in the starting position and waits for the starter's gun. She has the same intense focus in her eyes as Michael.

'Who is that?' I say.

'That's Mikayla,' Michael says. 'She's my twin sister.' As the starter pulls the trigger and the race begins, we watch Mikayla explode out of the blocks.

The script doesn't help me prepare for what I'm about to see. Mikayla's strides are graceful and elegant, but most of all, she is a blur of speed. After only the first 50 metres, it's easy to see she's the fastest in her race.

In fact, she might be **faster than her brother.**

Teddy's Tips No. 6

Run like the wind

Feel as light as the wind when you run. As soon as your feet touch the ground, pick them up. Use your arms and always look ahead to where you're running.

CHAPTER 7

NO GIRLS ALLOWED

It's been a while since the boys weren't talking to me. I didn't like how it made me feel, and I'm glad we've been able to patch things up. Until now, everything's been cool, but when Luke and I shared the news about spotting Michael and his sister Mikayla, Ben and Gerard weren't happy.

'NO WAY.

We can't have girls on our team,' said Gerard.

'She couldn't play our standard of footy,' said Ben.

I was excited when they shared their news about finding a kid called Connor at the basketball courts and I thought they would be excited about the twins as well. I guess I was wrong. Michael told us that he'd only play if Mikayla could play too. We're at risk of losing two of our fastest players just because Gerard and Luke don't want Mikayla on the team. I look to my Sydney Roosters team poster on the back of my bedroom door for guidance, but all I get in return is 18 players, one coach, two assistant coaches and three trainers smiling back at me. Thanks a lot, guys.

I get ready to type one of the hardest messages I've ever had to send. Being the captain means that I get most of the tough jobs. I tap away at the screen.

Hi Michael, really sorry but some of the boys reckon Mikayla couldn't handle being in the team. Hope you can still come. From Teddy.

My message has *Delivered* underneath it in small writing. Michael has read it and I wait for the three blinking dots that would tell me that he's replying, but they don't come. I check for the dots again. Not there. I check one more time. No dots, no nothing.

The Camden Rams rugby league fields are cold, damp and uninviting on Tuesday afternoon. Dad and I arrive 20 minutes early to set up the training gear. Once we're satisfied that the witches' hats, cones, tackling bags and balls are in place, Dad pulls out his flask of hot coffee and rubs his hands together while I get his clipboard from the car.

Walking back, I notice movement behind the small wooden grandstand that separates our training fields from Camden Red's. Their team has already made a start and I can see Shawn Sharpe leading his team around the ground for their warm-up. Behind him are Mohamed and Krispen, with the rest of the team following in a line like well-drilled soldiers. If we want to get close to beating Camden Red, we need to be better organised – and get more players.

All of a sudden, my hopes are answered.

'Teddy! Coach! Look what we've got!' Tawera and Dexter walk proudly up to Dad's car and dump their training bags on the soggy grass. They've got someone with them. Two people, in fact. Tawera and Dexter look like two little kids, bringing something exciting to school for Show and Tell.

'Who's this?' says Dad, taking a sip of hot black coffee. The two newcomers are both at least 40 centimetres taller than

Tawera and Dexter, not to mention twice as wide.

'This is Amiri and Soli,' says Tawera. 'We recruited them at KFC.'

FWOOSH!

Dad spits out his coffee in shock. Tawera and Dexter have to reach high to put their arms around the new recruits.

'KFC?' says Dad in surprise.

'Nah, kidding, Coach!' laughs Tawera. 'I mean at the park *across* from the KFC!'

'Do they have any skills?' asks Dad.

'They sure do, Coach,' says Dexter. 'They can tackle, offload and tackle some more!'

'Welcome to Camden Blue,' I say without hesitation. When we shake hands, mine are nearly crushed in their grip.

'Welcome to the front row, more like it!' says Dad, writing their names on the clipboard. 'Where are you guys from?'

'Cook Islands,' says Soli. 'We're cousins.'

'No, I mean, where do you live?'

'Oh, Rosemeadow,' says Soli. The introductions are interrupted when Ben and Gerard arrive. They also have someone with them.

'Yeah. More players!' bellows Tawera. The kid with Ben and Gerard has a basketball under his arm and is wearing a bright white

pair of Nike Air Jordans. He looks like he's just come from training. He glances around nervously.

'Hey, guys, this is Connor,' says Ben. 'He really wants to play, right, Connor?'

'Uh, yeah,' says Connor. He doesn't really look like he wants to be here. He looks down at the ground and doesn't make eye contact with anyone.

'You should see how quick he is with his hands, Coach,' says Gerard. 'We just need to teach him how to pass a footy.'

'I need to change my shoes,' Connor says softly, and walks over to the wooden grandstand. As Dad directs everyone to start stretching, I see Tobias and Patty arrive in the distance. Just like Luke and me, they've arrived empty-handed. Still, three new players are better than zero. We start with a calf stretch first and then move on to our hamstrings. It's important to stretch in this cold weather.

'Whoa! What the heck?' yells Tawera, stopping mid-stretch and pointing at the grandstand. The whole team turns their gaze to the steps of the grandstand where Connor, the new basketball kid, is sitting. At first, we don't know what's attracted Tawera's attention, but finally we see it. Instead of whispering or being polite, all the other members of Camden Blue run towards Connor for a closer look.

'Just make him feel welcome,' says Dad. 'You'll know what to do.' Before I can get to the grandstand, Tawera has started.

'Bro, what on earth?! You only have one foot?'

Poor Connor has gone red. It takes me a minute to work out what I'm seeing. He's holding a Nike basketball shoe but where one of his feet should be there's no foot. His leg finishes above his ankle.

'What happened to the other one?' Tawera asks.

Everyone is staring, waiting for Connor to answer.

'You don't have to tell us,' I say, stepping through the pack of nosy parkers. 'This is Connor's business, not ours,' I say to the boys.

Tawera looks guilty, and I can tell he didn't mean to embarrass Connor. He was just curious. We turn to walk back and finish our stretches.

'It's okay,' says Connor.

'IT'S NOT A SECRET.'

The team turn back around and wait eagerly for more.

'It's not that exciting,' explains Connor. 'I was born with one foot. Don't stress. I can run, step and jump just like everyone else. Maybe even higher than all of you.'

'What's in your other shoe if you only have one foot?' asks Luke. He asks what everyone else is thinking.

'A prosthetic,' says Connor, taking his other shoe out of his bag. Inside it is a shiny skin-coloured plastic foot.

'COOOOL!'

says the team. They've never seen a prosthetic foot before. Or leg. Or anything. Connor looks relieved at our reaction.

'If I want to play footy, all I need to do is change shoes, just like you guys,' he says. He rustles around in his gym bag and pulls out a pair of footy boots. He swaps them for his basketball shoes, ties them up tightly and runs over to Dad and starts his stretches.

'Can I stretch with you?' Gerard asks Connor.

'No, I want to stretch with him!' says Tawera. 'I was the one who discovered his foot!'

While Tawera and Gerard fight over who is going to stretch with Connor, Dad winks at me.

Finally, Camden Blue is starting to take shape.

Teddy's Tips No. 7

Don't look back

Whenever you feel regret, acknowledge it, and use it. Try not to let it consume you. Believe that you will become a better person because of the experience.

CHAPTER 8

HOLY CHICKEN McNUGGET

We're playing the Mount Annan Knights tonight.

We're only two players short, so we've got more of a chance against the Knights than we did against the Moss Vale Dragons. Two players short doesn't count for an interchange bench, which means we have a run-on team of 11. Two weeks ago we had to borrow players from our opposition, but something tells me that tonight we won't need to.

How do I know? Because of what happened today.

1. Mum picked me and Matt up from school.

2. When we stopped at the traffic lights on Gregory Hills Drive, a big black crow landed on the back of the council truck in front of us. It stared at me, through the windscreen and into my soul. I know this crow. It's connected to Percy Kelly, the regional selector.

3. When the traffic light turned green, the truck moved forward and gave the crow a fright. It flapped its wings and launched itself high into the air, but didn't take its eyes off me. I craned my neck to keep it in my sights.

4. As we turned the corner onto Camden Valley Way, the traffic slowed again. We came to a stop outside McDonald's. The crow dive-bombed towards our car, levelled out gracefully at the last minute and glided up towards the big yellow 'M' near the drive-through.

5. The traffic sped up and Mum accelerated past Maccas. The crow stayed on the big 'M', watching me as we turned the corner, then it was out of sight.

6. I was left with a good feeling. Something positive was coming.

As usual, Dad and I are the first ones at the ground. Mum, Nonno, Nonna and Matt will arrive closer to kick-off.

'Can you fill the water buckets, mate?' asks Dad. 'I'm just going to ask the Knights' coach if we can steal some of their players.'

The thought goes through my head. Two players who don't know how we play. Two players who don't really want to be there. Two players who might make mistakes just to help their mates on the other team win.

'Dad?' I call out.

'Yeah?' he says, stopping and turning around.

'Don't,' I tell him. 'We don't need them.'

Dad gives me a puzzled look.

'Mate, we only have eleven players. We don't want to get pumped again,' he says.

Water splashes over the edge of the half-filled water bucket and down my dark blue footy sock as I grip the handle and lower it to the ground, next to the basket of empty drink bottles.

'We'll be okay, Dad, I promise,' I say, not exactly knowing how I can make such a prediction.

'But you were so upset after we lost last time,' he says.

He's right. But my Spidey senses are telling me something else.

'I can't explain it, Dad,' I say. I even try my best to smile, just to make him feel better, but all it does is freak him out even more. 'All I know is that I have a feeling that everything will work out,' I finish.

Dad lets out an exasperated sigh.

'Whatever you think, son.' He shrugs. 'What would I know? I'm only the coach.' He sees President Taber walk out of the footy club and over to the canteen. 'You right with the water, James?' says Dad. 'I'm going to have a coffee with El Presidente.'

I nod and start filling up the drink bottles. As I fill the last bottle and place it in the basket, I feel a presence behind me. When I turn around, the traffic lights, the crow, the council truck and the big 'M' at McDonald's all come flooding back to me.

'Holy Chicken McNugget!' I say. I have no other words.

'What?' says the kid in front of me.

'Holy mother of Big Mac sauce!'

Again, the kid squints at me like I'm speaking another language, which I kind of am.

'What's with you and the McDonald's stuff?' he asks.

I try to speak, but I can't.

'It's you!' I finally say.

'Don't you dare call me Ronald McDonald,' he says. There's a girl next to him. She looks at me and the funny look on my face, and then back at him. She laughs.

'It's you! It's actually you!' I yell. Then I recognise his sister.

'AND YOU AS WELL!'

Now both of them are laughing. It's the twins from the athletics track. That wise old crow was sending me a message. He landed on the big 'M' for a reason: he was trying to tell me not to worry because Michael and Mikayla would be here! I quickly remember the text I sent Michael after Gerard and Ben said they didn't want a girl on the team. 'Hey, Michael. I never heard back from you.'

'That's because I told him not to reply,' says Mikayla. In an instant, she's gone from laughing to serious. It's clear she means business, and that she doesn't want her brother speaking on her behalf. 'I've been wanting to play footy for years,' she says, 'but all the local girls' teams are full!'

She crosses her arms and moves her head from side to side. It looks like she's thinking,

BOOM, TAKE THAT.

'Besides, I scare them too much,' she adds, pointing her finger at me and adding another head wobble.

'Hey, it's the twins!' says Luke, arriving before I get into more trouble with Mikayla. 'You playing for us or what?' Before Michael can speak, Mikayla takes over again.

'That's the plan,' she says. 'But if there's no me, there's no Michael – right, bruz?'

'Uh, yeah, sis,' says Michael, looking a bit embarrassed.

Tawera, Patty, Tobias and Dexter arrive.

'Hey, fellas, meet Mikayla and Michael,' says Luke. 'They're the twins from the athletics track we told you about.'

'You gonna be in our team?' says Tawera.

Before I can say anything, Mikayla pounces on Tawera's invitation.

'Don't mind if we do,' she says, and Michael grins.

'Deadly!' he says. 'Let's get our boots from the car.'

As the twins race off, I realise we now have another two players. We haven't got any reserves, but we have a full run-on squad.

Teddy's Tips No. 8

Back your instinct

Follow your intuition.

Take note of everything that is happening around you.

CHAPTER 9

THE FASTEST HUMAN EVER

Without any hesitation, Dad has the paperwork and sign-on sheet in front of the twins.

They lean the forms against the outside wall of our dressing sheds and fill them out with black pen.

'Are you sure about this, James?' Dad whispers to me from inside the doorway.

'Very sure,' I whisper back. 'Just go with me on this, Dad.'

After they've finished, Michael and Mikayla walk into the change rooms with their bags. Patty has his shirt off and as usual, he's flexing his muscles in the mirror. He sees Mikayla in the reflection and squeezes his biceps a little harder. She ignores him and drops her bag next to Gerard, who has entered through the other door with Ben. Gerard is tying up his bootlaces. Mikayla's aqua-green Nike bag takes him by surprise. I try to get in early and explain what's happened, but I'm not quick enough.

'Never seen a **GIRL** before?'

says Mikayla. Gerard just sits there staring, looking stunned.

'Is this the girl from Little Athletics, Teddy?' he says.

I nod.

'I thought we weren't playing her?' says Gerard.

'I'm right here,' says Mikayla, getting in Gerard's face. 'I *can* hear you, you know.'

'Yeah, Teddy,' says Ben. 'I thought you told them that there are no girls allowed?'

'Let's make a deal,' says Mikayla, her voice calm as she eyeballs Gerard. 'You and me, out on the field, right now. Hundred-metre sprint, tryline to tryline. You win? I leave. I win? You shut up and let me play.'

A stone-cold silence comes over the change room, except for the sound of Dad coming in, slurping on his coffee.

'Do it!' says Dad.

'Do it! Do it! Do it!' Tawera chants.

Soon enough, the whole team joins in.

'DO IT! DO IT!

DO IT!'

they sing.

'Serious?' Gerard laughs, looking at Mikayla like she's a walkover.

I decide not to say anything and let it all play out.

'Deadly serious,' she answers.

'Okay then,' he says. 'You're on.'

The team follow Mikayla and Gerard out of the change rooms and onto the field. Camden Red are finishing their game against the Narellan Jets.

We all stop at the sideline, but Gerard and Mikayla walk onto the field, with the game being played around them. People are yelling at them to get off the field, but mentally, they are in the zone. Finally, they reach the tryline directly under the goalposts.

'This will be a walk in the park,' says Gerard.

'Don't walk, whatever you do,' says Mikayla, smiling. 'On the count of three, we start here and we finish at the other end. Okay?'

Gerard nods and looks over at us, smirking. Camden Red and Narellan are still battling it out around them.

Mikayla counts to three and they explode forward. Mikayla glides over the dew-soaked evening grass effortlessly, but Gerard looks like he's trying hard to keep up. He grits his teeth and looks over at Mikayla, her legs blurring like the Road Runner, but her face is calm and composed. Gerard pumps his arms to try and get more speed but it's no use. Mikayla is like an F-15 fighter jet moving at the speed of sound. By the time she hits the other end, Gerard is only just past halfway.

We go nuts! Mikayla is the fastest human we have ever seen! Even Camden Red and Narellan have stopped mid-play to admire Mikayla's speed.

To his credit, once he gets to her, Gerard reaches out and shakes Mikayla's hand.

'I was wrong,' he puffs. 'You're going to be great. Are you a school champion?'

'No,' says Mikayla as they walk back to us on the sideline. 'New South Wales Under 12s champion.'

The current game's fulltime siren fills the air. It's time to get Mikayla and Michael their jerseys.

Back in the change rooms, we're ready to play, but Dad has made some last-minute changes. He finishes scribbling on the whiteboard and spins it around to face us. We sit on the cold wooden benches, boots laced, mouthguards in and focused.

'Okay, team, listen up,' he says. His gumboots squelch on the tiles of the dressing shed as he shifts position to point at the new version of the team list on the whiteboard. 'I've made some quick changes. Read it carefully, especially our new players,' he says.

1.	Fullback	James Tedesco
2.	Wing	Michael Malone
3.	Centre	Tobias Paulo
4.	Centre	Tawera Richardson
5.	Wing	Mikayla Malone
6.	Five-eighth	Connor Ellis
7.	Halfback	Gerard Quig
8.	Front Row	Soli Puna
9.	Hooker	Ben Sarkis
10.	Front Row	Amiri Puna
11.	Second Row	Luke Pollard
12.	Second Row	Dexter Collins
13.	Lock	Patty Daly

'Notice anything?' asks Dad after we've all had time to read our positions.

'Your handwriting is very neat for an old person?' suggests Ben.

'Besides that,' says Dad, rolling his eyes. He waits for an answer but there isn't one, only crickets. 'We have no reserves,' Dad finally says. 'We have a run-on team, which is great, but if anyone wants to come off, we'll be short – okay?'

Everyone nods. We're just happy to have 13 players for once.

'Now, get out there and have fun!' yells Dad. 'You've got this!'

When I look around the shed and see:

- **three of my best friends, Ben, Luke and Gerard**
- **Patty with freshly combed hair**
- **Tawera with a cheeky smile**

- **Tobias and Dexter strapping up their headgear**
- **Soli and Amiri, the Cook Islander cousins**
- **Connor, who won't let a prosthetic foot stop him from playing footy and . . .**

the lightning bolt twins, Mikayla and Michael

I finally feel like this is my team. Our team. Just like Dad said – we've got this!

Teddy's Tips No. 9

Game day routine

Make sure you have plenty of rest the night before. Try to relax and not waste energy thinking about the game. I walk or swim before I play.

CHAPTER 10

DOGS ON A SAUSAGE

It takes a while for the new players to adjust to their positions. Each time Mount Annan scores, it's because someone has moved infield too quickly or not moved out fast enough. It's 15 minutes into the first half with five minutes to go. We're huddled under the goalposts and Mount Annan have scored again. Mount Annan lead Camden Blue 10–0. If the scoring continues like this, it will end up like our game against the Moss Vale Dragons.

'Mikayla, I need you to do something,' I say.

Mikayla lowers the drink bottle she's sipping and raises her eyebrows.

'I need you to stay on your wing,' I say. 'If you come off your wing, you're leaving space for them to score.'

I think I've poked the hornet's nest. The look on her face says it all.

'Well, Captain Big Ted,' she says, 'you better give me the ball so I feel like I'm involved. I didn't join the team just to make up the numbers.'

She has a point. Maybe we do need to spice up our attack.

'Fine,' I say. 'Next time the backs have the ball, you and me will work the right side of the field.'

Mount Annan kick the conversion, which takes the score to 12–0. Before we head back to halfway, I have one more thing to say. 'Soli and Amiri, can you force a mistake after kick-off?'

'For sure, Teddy,' says Amiri with fire in his eyes.

Gerard kicks off and the ball travels deep into Mount Annan territory. Before I can see which player will receive it, Amiri and Soli come tearing past me like two wild bulls. *Oh no,* I think. *This is going to hurt.* The Mount Annan lock forward runs the ball up bravely, but the impact of the human tsunami soon buries him in the ground. Instantly the ball comes loose.

'Hey, Teddy, we did it!'

says Soli, fist-pumping the air.

'That's great, but dive on the ball!' I yell. So he does.

Ben runs into the dummy half position behind Soli and fires the ball out to me.

'You ready, Mikayla?' I say, running towards her wing. She nods.

The Mount Annan defence, still scrambling, follow me across the field and get ready for the famous Tedesco step.

Instead, I pop an easy ball up for Mikayla.

'Finally,' she says, gripping the footy in her hands. Mikayla's opposite winger moves up quickly to tackle her, but she sticks out her palm and flicks him off like a mozzie. Mikayla then steps in to draw their centre, then steps back out at a speed no one is prepared for. She moves the ball to her other hand and tucks it under her arm as she hits some space.

The Mount Annan fullback is flying across the field but he has no chance. In fact, Mikayla has so much room to move, she curves back infield and scores a try under the posts. The Camden crowd goes bananas at the strength, skill and speed they have just witnessed. Michael is the first player in to congratulate her.

'Nice work, sis,' he says as he gives her a high-five.

'See? I'm not here to make up the numbers, Teddy,' she says to me.

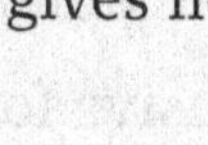

'That was amazing,' I say.

She sticks her hand up for a high-five, but I grip it instead and shake her hand properly.

'Welcome to the team, Mikayla,' I say.

'Just hurry up and kick the conversion, Teddy,' she says, smiling. 'We've got a game to win.'

Finally, we've broken the ice.

The scoreboard is now 12–6, Mount Annan leading with five minutes to go in the first half. This time the Mount Annan Knights kick off to us and the red and blue jerseys chase it like dogs on a hot sausage.

'Mine!' yells Patty as the ball hits the ground and grubbers towards him. Patty picks it up skilfully after an awkward bounce and, knowing that we'd like one more try before halftime, he runs hard at the Mount Annan defenders, who are already in a tight defensive formation. Again, Ben moves into the dummy half position as Patty is tackled and plays the ball.

'Forwards, hit the line!' I scream as Camden Blue prepare to attack. Luke runs first. He barrels into three defenders, not taking a backward step. 'Who's next?' I yell.

'Me, me, me!' says Amiri, getting Ben's attention.

Again, Ben pops up a ball as Amiri hustles forward like a wrecking ball, making valuable metres and taking at least four defenders with him.

'Give the forwards one more run and then it's the backs' ball!' I command.

Dexter takes control and runs off Ben, catching the scrambling defence by surprise with his speed. He crosses halfway and hits the 40-metre mark before being tackled around the legs and crashing to the ground.

'Gerard, left is wide open!' I shout. From the position of fullback, I can see everything. If Gerard finds space for our players on the left-hand side, we can score. This time Gerard scoots from dummy half and our backs are already reading his mind.

Tobias runs a decoy move, crossing infield and bringing two defenders with him. Gerard spots the mistake that Mount Annan makes and shoots a straight ball to Michael, hitting him right on the chest. Like his sister, Michael speeds ahead gracefully, stepping one defender and another. As the Mount Annan fullback closes in on Michael, Connor appears from nowhere.

'Yes, Michael, next to you!' he screams.

Without even looking, Michael flicks a trick pass behind his back and Connor successfully catches it while running at full pace. He clutches the ball carefully in his hands and runs another ten metres to score in the corner.

Again, the crowd stands up!

'Ladies and gentlemen, we have a game on our hands!' says the ground announcer on the microphone. 'Two of Camden Blue's newest recruits, Michael Malone and

Connor Ellis, combine to take the score to 12 points to 10. Mount Annan still in front!'

The halftime siren echoes off the grandstand as I walk back to take the conversion.

'Don't miss it, Teddy!' jeers someone from the stands.

'Yeah, this is a REALLY hard kick!' someone else laughs.

I should know better, but I look up to see who it is. Shawn, Krispen

and the rest of my old team, Camden Red, are watching the game. Usually they would shower and go home after their match, but there's a buzz around the ground about the new-look Camden Blue.

As I place the ball on the kicking tee, I do everything I can to block them out. I can't let them get into my head.

I look over to Dad, who is giving me the thumbs up.

I gaze over at the other stand where Nonna is holding up her well-worn Go Teddy! sign.

'DON'T SLIP!'

yells Shawn. He's pulling out all the stops to put me off my game.

I move five steps forward, then five steps back.

Then I run forward and follow through on the kick.

GO TEDDY!

As my foot connects with the ball, I know it feels wrong.

I've missed the conversion.

The ball swings inside the posts and we remain on ten points. We only have one half left to play.

This game will go down to the wire, and my unsuccessful conversion might have lost it for us.

I've let everyone down.

Teddy's Tips No. 10

Fending off

Use the fend when trying to get away from a defender: stiff arm, open hand, and push off the defender's chest with your free hand.

CHAPTER 11

HANG IN THERE

We're tired.

Cooked.
Gassed.
Exhausted.

With no reserves, we've kept the score to 12–10.

There are only 12 minutes to go in the second half.

Mount Annan's attack is relentless and they've completed at least three sets of six

down our end of the field. Our defence is courageous, but the cracks are starting to appear.

'Communicate!' I yell. 'Say which player you're marking!'

'I can't breathe, Teddy!' gasps Soli. 'Can I have a rest?'

'No, Soli! I need you to hang in there!' I say.

He nods and wipes the sweat pouring off his forehead onto his jersey. The Mount Annan attackers can see that Soli is vulnerable and run the ball at him. He's slow on his feet and dives to tackle their runner but grasps at thin air. The Mount Annan player moves towards the right of the field with nearly his whole team in support.

'Mikayla, come across and help!' I scream.

As Mikayla flies across the field, it's up to me and her to stop them from scoring.

'Stay on those two!' I say. 'I'll take these three!'

But the maths doesn't work to our advantage. Five players on two players means that we're greatly outnumbered. Mount Annan zigzag the ball across their five attackers until their winger finds our weak spot. He speeds ahead in an unmarked part of the field and scores an easy try under the goalposts. Mount Annan rush in and celebrate, surrounding their scoring player.

'Sorry, Teddy,' says Mikayla. Her hands are on her hips and she's puffing.

'We were outnumbered,' I say.

The rest of Camden Blue jog up the field and I can see they're dead on their feet. This time, Soli's not the only one whose lungs are burning.

'Come on, guys – hang in there!' I plead. 'You're all playing so well.'

The Mount Annan kicker is lining up for his conversion from right in front.

'If he kicks this, tonight is over for us,' Tobias says despondently. A few of the others murmur in agreement.

'No way, it's not even close to being over,' says a soft voice behind me. It's Luke. I'm the only one who has heard him. I'm waiting for him to do a stirring victory speech, but when I turn around, he's distracted by something in the grandstand.

'What did you say?' I ask. This time Luke repeats himself, but is ten times louder than before.

'GUYS, IT'S NOT EVEN CLOSE TO BEING OVER!' he screams, pointing directly into the grandstand. 'BREEANNA, THIS GAME IS FOR YOU!' he yells.

The Mount Annan player's kick is successful, but we're all looking at Breeanna sitting in the grandstand, next to Rocco, her family's prize-winning goat. GO LUKE is painted in large blue letters on Rocco's side.

'Mount Annan increase their lead,' echoes the ground announcer's voice from the loudspeakers. 'Mount Annan 18, Camden Blue 10.'

'Eight minutes to go,' says Luke, half looking at us while half looking back at Breeanna. Or Rocco. Or both of them. Rocco's looking straight at Luke, which is a little bit freaky. 'We can still win this – we just need to get ten points,' he says.

Easier said than done, but Luke's right.

We *can* win this.

'Gerard, your turn to kick. Aim low, grubber if possible, please,' I say as we run back to halfway. 'Luke, I'll chase and you run support, okay?'

'Got it,' says Luke.

'Channel your energy into scoring a try,' I say. 'Breeanna will love you for it!'

'Will she ever!' says Luke with the biggest grin. He spins around like someone in love in one of those old-fashioned black and white movies.

'What the heck is wrong with him?' asks Gerard with a look of bewilderment on his face.

'Just go with it,' I say. 'Remember, grubber kick.'

Gerard does exactly that, and the ball ricochets off the side of his foot and bounces aggressively along the ground, making it extremely hard to pick up. With all the speed I can muster, I track the ball like a ballistic missile, following each bump, angle and turn that it takes. Finally, as the ball makes one last bounce upward towards the Mount Annan fullback, I also make a challenge for it and clasp it cleanly in my hands.

'Camden Blue takes possession!' yells the referee.

Their fullback reacts quickly and grips me tightly around the waist, but sure enough, Luke is right there next to me, just like I asked him to be.

'I've got you on the right, Teddy!' Luke yells.

I spin in the tackle and pass to Luke, who is nearly unmarked. He catches it and moves quickly upfield, the cover defence closing in on him fast.

'I'M OPEN!'

yells Mikayla. Luke knows he's about to be tackled, so he throws a clean ball to Mikayla, who's staying just inside the white paint of the sideline. The same defenders who were zeroing in on Luke now move towards her. If she gets tackled, they will send her into touch. If she passes, Luke is now open and can score. Mikayla draws them across as far as she safely can. Just as they commit to the tackle, she lollipops a high ball over to Luke, above the defenders' heads. The ball floats backwards and lands gently in Luke's hands. He's the only person in sight of the tryline and he dives over, right under the goalposts.

Camden Blue rush in to congratulate our scorer but he's already running towards the fence separating the field from the spectators. In a flash he's balancing on the fence, making a love-heart shape with his hands over his chest and smiling up at Breeanna. Then he points at her and does a backflip off the fence, landing back on the playing field.

The familiar voice of the ground announcer fills the air again. 'Luke Pollard, playing second row for Camden Blue, scores a magnificent try! Love is in the air, folks!'

With no time to waste, I kick the conversion. Shawn and his mates are on the other side of the field, so this time I don't hear their nonsense. Four minutes to go. The scoreboard lights up on top of the western grandstand as we race back to our positions, ready to receive the ball from Mount Annan again.

Camden Blue 16 – Visitors 18
Time remaining:
04 minutes 10 seconds

This time it's a short kick-off that only goes 20 metres. Tawera isn't expecting it. The ball floats across the field to him at centre, but as he jumps to catch it, he is challenged by Mount Annan's winger. Arms and legs windmill through the air, but the Mount Annan winger is too quick this time. He crashes to the ground with the ball and Mount Annan get the sniff of another try. I can see their hooker behind the winger about to play the ball. The hooker is ready to scoot forward and catch us off guard.

'He's going to run, watch him!' I yell. Fortunately, Luke senses the hooker's move as well. Luke, now with the wind in his sails, races up on their hooker and completes a one-on-one strip. With the stolen ball in his hands, Luke moves sideways and tries to run up the centre of the field, but he's stopped quickly by a wall of strong Mount Annan forwards. They drive him into the damp grass, but he hangs on to the ball. Unfazed, he springs to his feet.

'I'm okay!' he yells out to Breeanna. 'Don't worry about me!'

'Hurry up and play the ball, dude,' Ben says behind him. Two minutes on the clock.

Amiri gets the first run and rumbles forward like a steam train, skittling the defence until they hang on desperately and he finally trips over the players underneath him. I scan the field in front of me, looking for an opportunity or a gap to run at. Finally, I see half a chance between their five-eighth and centre. I whistle over at Mikayla. She raises her eyebrows to indicate she's already seen what I have. Game on.

'Mine, Ben, mine!' I yell, leaping out of position and brushing past our forwards like a rude kid jumping the queue at McDonald's. Ben throws the ball and I have a Spidey senses moment with a game of join-the-dots:

– Run at the centre and throw a dummy towards Mikayla / Step left. ***Dot joined.***

– Put the ball under my other arm and fend their five-eighth as he moves in / Watch him faceplant. ***Dot joined.***

– Angle my run inward and call for

Mikayla to follow on the outside / Draw their winger off the line. ***Dot joined.***

– When the winger has created a gap in defence and is running at me, pass to Mikayla. ***Dot joined.***

– Watch Mikayla run a sharp angle infield and outrun their fullback. He has no chance. Mikayla sprints like her life depends on it. She dives under the posts and scores, sliding across the slippery grass. ***Mission accomplished!***

It's Camden Blue 20, Mount Annan 18!

The boys rush in and crowd Mikayla. Dad's so happy he's doing the 'Macarena' again on the sideline. I rush back and set up for the kick. I know I can kick this one with my eyes closed. I can hear the boos and comments coming from Shawn and his Camden Red crew, but this time it's in one ear and out the other.

The ball sails between the posts with only 30 seconds to go. When Mount Annan kick off, we hold the ball as if our lives depend on it, and the score stays at 22–18. When the fulltime siren sounds, we all realise: we've won our first game as Camden Blue!

Dad runs onto the field and hugs us all. It feels like we've won the grand final even though it's just a normal round game. It feels so good because for the first time, we've played like a team and believed in ourselves.

In fact, if we can keep this up, we might even have a chance of beating Camden Red.

Teddy's Tips No. 11

Sidestepping

Shift your weight through the leg you're stepping off, press off the inside off your foot and push through the ground to beat a defender. Always maintain balance, and keep your eyes on the defender.

CHAPTER 12

DOG'S BUTT, BATMAN & ROBIN

Lewis and I are at the mall again.

We peer around the corner near the Donut King entry to make sure no one's watching, then use the service lift to travel down to the bottom level of the basement.

So far, our hiding spot for the 3D printer has kept Lewis out of trouble at home, and the best part is that he's been busy printing off a heap of Stealth-Stud soles. The darkest corner of the basement

looks like a mad scientist's laboratory, with the 3D printer, tools, power cords and spotlights spread across the concrete floor. In one of the Batman movies, Bruce Wayne and Lucius Fox keep all of Batman's gadgets in an underground bunker like this.

Well, if I'm Batman, then Lewis is Robin. Or maybe it's the other way around. Lewis is running this show.

Lewis reaches up and puts his hand in a hidden nook within the concrete wall next to the service lift. 'Check these out,' he says.

He's holding a 3D printout of our Stealth-Stud design. The studs and sole are fluoro orange, just like the ones that the NRL players use. Lewis is displaying them like they are valuable gemstones. And just like diamonds, the tips of the studs shine in the glow of the spotlights that Lewis is using to illuminate the basement.

'No way!' I gasp. 'They are awesome!'

'Aren't they just,' Lewis says with a satisfied look on his face. For a minute, we stand in silence, admiring the Stealth Studs, like Willy Wonka inspecting one of his delicious creations in the chocolate factory. The silence is broken by a noise in the distance. It's probably a car door closing in the carpark above us.

'So how do we turn these into a proper footy boot?' I ask.

'What do you mean?' says Lewis.

'Well, these are just the soles – the bottom of the shoe,' I say. 'They need to be attached to the part you put your foot in and lace up.'

The penny drops and Lewis realises that we are only halfway there. Lewis is great at the scientific side of things, but I'm good at making it all come together.

'Any ideas?' asks Lewis, shrugging.

'Miss Warren will help us,' I say. 'She is sure to have some advice about how we can design the top half.'

The same sound as before echoes through the cool air of the basement.

But this time it's louder.

We spin around towards the fire exit door, which is in the dim back corner of the basement. Three dark shadows are standing in front of it. As they come closer and cross the beam of the spotlights, I recognise them.

'Pssst, hide the Stealth Studs,' I whisper. Lewis shoves them behind his back.

The shadowy figures are now in full view. They squint at us through the brightness of the lights shining in their eyes.

'Turn those lights on them, not us!' instructs the one in the middle. It's Damir, the trolley boy, and two of his trolley boy gang members. The one with the patchy beard who Gerard called Dog's Butt spins the spotlight stand around so the lights are shining directly on us instead.

We look like we're in one of those movies where the baddies are being interrogated by the cops.

'Well, well, well,' sneers Damir. 'It's Loser Number Two who was helping Loser Number One steal my girlfriend.'

He steps closer and looks around the basement. 'And what's going on here?' he asks menacingly.

I can hear Lewis breathing. He's scared. He doesn't like conflict.

'Nothing,' I say. 'Just helping the janitor with some jobs.'

'LIAR!'

hisses Damir.

He steps forward and punches me in the stomach.

I'm winded and fall to my knees. I can hear Damir's mates laughing as I gasp for air. It's the worst pain in the world.

'Do you want some of that too?' Damir says to Lewis.

'N-N-NO,'

stutters Lewis.

I get up on one knee and raise my head to see Damir walking over to the school's 3D printer and running his greasy fingers over it.

'What's this?' he says, looking back at us. 'I bet it's worth some decent coin.'

Before I can make something up and tell him it's worthless, like a computerised apple peeler, Lewis comes clean.

'It's a 3D printer that lets you print anything you want,' he blurts out.

Damir smiles, showing his yellow teeth, which are stained from too many energy drinks.

'I've heard of those,' says Dog's Butt. 'You can print your own weapons and fake credit cards.'

I'm not surprised it's the illegal items he homes in on. It's not like he'd use it to make a vase for some flowers or a bookmark.

'We'll take it then,' says Damir. 'Thanks for your generosity.'

'Hey, that's not yours!' I say, finally getting back on my feet. Damir begins to walk over.

'Want another one of these?' he asks, holding up his fist.

'Just take it,' says Lewis. 'Please don't hurt my friend again.'

They all laugh and the sound bounces off the concrete floor and walls of the basement. Dog's Butt unplugs the printer and hefts it up under his arm.

'Don't hurt my friend,' he mimics as they saunter back to the fire escape.

When they're gone, we slump to the ground. I'm still in pain and Lewis is crying.

'Are you okay?' I ask.

Lewis doesn't answer for a bit. He sniffs and wipes his eyes on the back of his hand.

'What are we going to tell Miss Warren? And I should have stuck up for you,' he says. 'I should have done something, but I was scared.'

'It's okay,' I say. 'There were three of them and –'

'It's not okay!' Lewis interrupts. He's not angry with me, he's angry with himself. 'Look at the size of me! You're braver than I am and I'm twice as big as you!'

I place a hand on his shoulder.

'It really is okay, Lewis,' I say. 'You just need to build your self-confidence, that's all.'

'Shame!' He sniffles. 'And how do I do that?'

'You mean build self-confidence?' I ask him.

'Yeah,' he says.

'I have an idea,' I say. 'Are you free on Tuesday afternoon?'

Teddy's Tips No. 12

Dummy passes

You have to convince a defender you are going to throw a real pass so set up a dummy pass just like a real one. Hold the ball out in front before shaping to throw the pass.

CHAPTER 13

ARMPIT STINK

Sometimes I'm my own worst enemy. If I make a mistake on the field, I think about it morning, noon and night. It replays in my head so much that sometimes I find it hard to get to sleep. Last night was no different. Even though we beat Mount Annan yesterday, I can't get my missed conversion out of my mind. I'm not cranky at Shawn or Krispen for putting me off; I'm cranky at myself for letting them get to me.

The sun is beginning to creep through my curtains. I rub my eyes and estimate that I've only had a few hours' sleep. We play Camden Red next weekend. I can't go into the game doubting my kicking ability. I also can't prepare for such an important game with so little sleep. I decide to use one of my strategies that helps me deal with my overthinking. This morning I'm going to take control. Right now. This very instant. At five-thirty in the morning.

I throw off my warm Roosters doona and strap on my boots. They click-clack as I walk down the hallway towards my brother Matthew's room. His door is closed and has a DO NOT ENTER sign that he found on the ground near the old Menangle footy fields. Under the sign is a Parramatta Eels team poster with big globs of Blu Tack sticking out at the corners. I ignore the sign and turn the doorhandle. Matt's room stinks of dirty socks.

'Matt!' I say. 'I need to do kicking practice. Want to play Best Out of Ten?' He mumbles something and turns over on his stomach, shoving the pillow over his head. 'Matt! I know you can hear me,' I say to him, walking over his dirty socks and undies which are strewn across his floor like landmines. I poke him in the shoulder until he takes the pillow off his head.

'Dude! The sun isn't even up yet!' he finally says, squinting at me.

'I didn't sleep, Matt. I tried, but I couldn't,' I say.

He sees that I'm wearing pyjamas and footy boots. He knows that I'm serious.

'I won't be able to relax until I kick some conversions.'

'This is about the one you missed, right?' Matt sighs. He throws his legs out of the bed and plants his feet on the floor. He sits on the side of the bed for a while, rubbing his eyes and trying to wake up.

'So, Best Out of Ten?' I ask him again.

'Yeah, okay,' he says. 'Go and set the balls up. I'll be outside soon.'

Best brother ever!

I click-clack down the hallway again, race outside and get the gear from the tractor shed. It's time to get my kick on.

I'm ready to go. The grass on the practice paddock is freshly mown and wet with dew. The early-morning fog drifts across the farm and the cows at the other end of the paddock are watching me curiously as I stretch my calves and hamstrings. Matt appears at the front door and warms his hands with his breath. Steam rises up from his hands with each exhalation. He's slipped on a tracksuit and his Parramatta beanie. Like me, he's got his boots on.

'Hey, let's make this a bit different today,' I say to him. He looks at the balls spaced evenly across the field and then at the goalposts. To Matt, it appears to be a normal game of Best Out of Ten.

'Different how?' he asks.

'Each time I'm about to kick, I want you to try and put me off,' I say.

'Like those kids the other night?' he says.

'Yep, exactly like that,' I say. 'Yell out something dumb.'

I move over to the first ball and place it on the kicking tee. The first kick will be from the left-hand side of the field. I'm already beginning to line up the kick when Matt yells out from behind the post.

'So you actually want me to yell out just as you're kicking?' he says.

'Yep.'

'Like what?' he asks.

'Be creative,' I say. Matt nods and I can tell he's trying to think of something clever to yell.

Again, I line up my kick. I take a deep breath and exhale. Like Matt, a cloud of steam exits my mouth in the cool Menangle morning air. I step back, then run forward and –

'WILLY WILLY WOMBAT!' Matt yells. This time I've anticipated that there will be noise and I totally block it. The ball flies cleanly off my foot and floats straight between the posts! One from one.

'Willy willy wombat?' I say to Matt. 'Really? Is that all you've got?' I laugh.

Matt takes this as a challenge. I line up the second kick. Again, I step back, then run forward –

'BOOGER BOOTS!'

he yells this time. Just as I kick, I giggle at the 'booger' part. Luckily, the ball still goes through the posts.

'Good kick!' Matt laughs. He thinks it's pretty funny too. Kick three coming up. I start to move in.

'ARMPIT STINK!' he sings. Again, I do my best to block it out and the ball sails through!

By the time I'm on the tenth kick, I've kicked nine from nine. Can I actually get ten in a row? I need to make this one count. If I'm finally going to push the other night's missed kick out of my mind once and for all, this kick will seal the deal. I look at the ball, then at the posts. Then at the ball again and at the posts again. I step back, then move forward and –

'DON'T FLASH YOUR BUTT RASH!' he yells. I can't believe it; the ball goes straight through. It's a perfect score, ten out of ten! The cows go wild! Matt runs over and high-fives me. 'Well done, little bro,' he says.

Matt doesn't usually give compliments, so I can tell that he's pretty impressed. I'm more impressed with the distractions he came up with. Especially the one about the butt rash.

'You ready for Camden Red?' he asks.

'As ready as I'll ever be,' I say. It feels like a weight has been lifted from my shoulders. Suddenly, a hearty chuckle in the distance gets our attention. As usual, Nonno has gone for his early-morning walk up to the top paddock. He takes his binoculars to look at the hot-air balloons as they drift above the farms in the district. This morning he's finding it hard to hold the binoculars up to his eyes because he's laughing so much.

'What the . . . ?' says Matt, looking up in the air for the nearest balloon, but all he can see is the sun rising in the east and some light wispy clouds overhead.

'Vieni a vedere!' shouts Nonno from the hill.

He's telling us to come and see.

Matt and I leave the footballs where they are and sprint up to Nonno's vantage point.

Still laughing, he hands Matt the binoculars and points towards the southern end of our property. I squint to try and see what's there, but whatever it is, it's too far away.

'No way!' gasps Matt, standing tall with the binoculars pressed up hard against his eyes. He starts to laugh. 'NO *WAY*!' By now he's lowered the binoculars and he's next to Nonno, sitting on the ground and heaving with laughter.

'Give me those!' I say, and yank the binoculars off him. I scan the area but can't see anything out of the ordinary.

'Just beyond those trees,' says Matt. 'At Breeanna's house.' That's when it comes into focus. In the front paddock there is a picnic blanket, all spread out with what looks like breakfast – croissants, toast and fresh fruit. Sitting and gazing into each other's eyes are Breeanna and Luke. He's even wearing his best shirt. It's the same one he wore to his cousin's wedding last year. They're sipping hot drinks and probably telling each other how in love they are. Behind them, their breakfast is getting cold and is slowly disappearing.

That's what happens when you bring a goat on a picnic date.

Breathe through it

Things don't always go to plan so take the time to reset and stay focused. If you are feeling overwhelmed, take three deep breaths and focus on your breathing.

CHAPTER 14

THE SCIENCE  LESSON 

'Come on, James, help me out!' pleads Dad over dinner.

'Two reserves, that's all I'm asking for.' Dad knows that this weekend's game may as well be the grand final. We're playing Camden Red, and just like me, Dad wants to prove a point by not just beating them, but by whooping their boastful butts.

Mum's getting a bit cranky with Dad because he's taking this game so seriously and putting pressure on me to find two new players.

'John Tedesco!' Mum says. She places her fork next to her plate of chicken cacciatore. When Mum says your first *and* last name and then puts her fork down at the dinner table, you know things are going to get real.

Judging by the look on Dad's face, he's just realised that Mum's about to unload.

'James is under enough pressure to captain this team to a win against Camden Red!'

Dad tries to say something but Mum shuts him down. 'He doesn't need the extra worry of signing up more new players, does he?'

'No, dear,' Dad says. He looks down at his plate and scoops up some chicken and tomato sauce on his fork. Mum studies him, just to make sure he looks remorseful enough before she picks up her fork again. She must decide he does, because she continues eating. Dad looks over and gives Matt and me a quick wink.

'It's okay, Mum,' I say. 'I think I know someone who wants to play.'

Dad nearly chokes on his chicken when he hears my news.

'Really?' he asks, clearing his throat. 'Who?'

'Lewis from school,' I reply.

'Whoa!' says Matt.

'Yep,' I say.

Matt starts to get excited.

'If you reckon Soli and Amiri are big, Dad, you should see Lewis!' says Matt.

'Is he any good?' asks Dad.

'He will be,' I say. 'After I teach him how to pass the ball, run the ball, tackle and be tackled.'

'So, you're saying he's got potential?' says Dad. He's a glass-half-full kind of guy.

'Heaps of potential!' I say.

On Tuesday after school, I meet Lewis at the training fields and make sure that he has told his parents about coming to footy training. There's no point keeping secrets from your mum and dad, they always find out the truth.

'I promised them that my studies won't suffer,' Lewis says. 'Besides, I said it would help with my self-confidence.'

I'm glad he listened to me. I suggest to Lewis that we work on some skills before the rest of the team arrives.

I throw the ball to him and he catches it.

Tick.

I ask him to pass it back. He does.

Tick.

I tell him to run at me. But he just stands there.

I tell him to run at me again. He still just stands there, frozen.

I wait.

And wait.

And wait.

And wait.

'What's the matter, Lewis? You're way bigger than me,' I tell him.

'I've never been tackled before,' he says.

'I won't hurt you,' I say.

'But what about in a real game?' he says. 'It won't be you tackling me.' He's right – I didn't think of that. Fortunately, I remember that Science is his favourite subject.

'Lewis, explain the science behind a pendulum.'

'That's easy, Teddy,' he says enthusiastically. 'Pendulums have energy in their systems. When the pendulum weight is lifted, it contains gravitational potential energy. When the weight is released, the potential energy is converted into kinetic energy, or energy of motion.'

'And what if a heavy pendulum weight hits a smaller pendulum weight?' I say. Lewis gets even more excited.

'Another easy one. I'll make it simple for

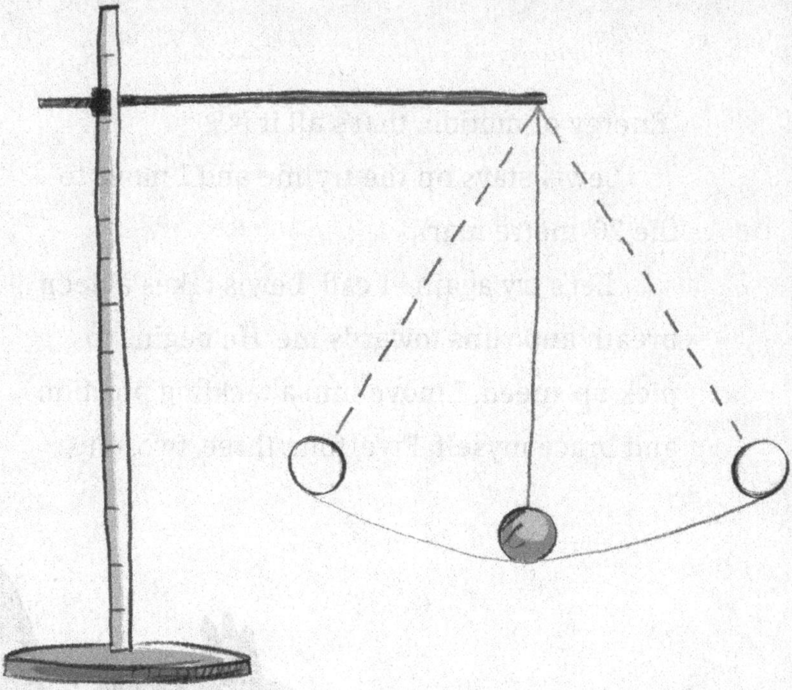

you – the smaller pendulum is sent flying.'

I get ready to finish the science lesson.

'Lewis – YOU BIG PENDULUM! YOU STRONG!' I say in a Tarzan voice.

Lewis laughs.

'TEDDY SMALL PENDULUM! TEDDY GET SENT INTO SPACE!'

Lewis laughs again and begins to loosen up.

'Okay, I get it,' he says, gripping the ball.

'Energy of motion, that's all it is.'

Lewis stays on the tryline and I move to the 20-metre mark.

'Let's try again,' I call. Lewis takes a deep breath and runs towards me. He begins to pick up speed. I move into a tackling position and brace myself. Five, four, three, two, one,

KABO

OOOM!

Lewis the big pendulum smashes Teddy the little pendulum to smithereens. I lie on my back and admire the stars. The only problem is that I'm seeing stars that aren't really there.

'Teddy?' says Lewis, looking down at me. He slaps me lightly on the cheeks. 'Teddy?' He squirts water from his drink bottle on my face. I quickly return to earth.

'What happened?' I say groggily. 'Did I tackle you?'

'Ah, you tried really hard,' Lewis says politely. 'But . . . I smashed you.'

He helps me to my feet. 'You going to be okay?' Lewis asks. It takes me a while to answer.

'Only if you promise to run like that on Friday night,' I say.

Teddy's Tips No. 14

The glass half full

Focus on your own and your team's potential instead of your limitations. You will feel more empowered and good things will happen when you give your energy to your strengths!

CHAPTER 15

CAMDEN BLUE IS DEAD

Alex arrives at school at the same time as Matt and me. He's juggling his soccer ball on his feet, knees and head.

'Hey, Teddy, wait up!' he yells as he sees me walking through the front gate.

'Catch ya later, little bro,' says Matt, walking off to the senior section of the school. 'See you at the game tonight.'

Our whole family is pumped for the showdown against Camden Red.

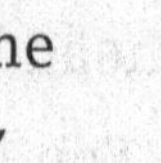

Dad pulled an all-nighter prepping for the game. He's organised the game plan and positions, and has some new plays written down. There's no way he wants to lose to Coach Sharpe and his son Shawn.

'You got your head in the zone?' asks Alex. 'Everyone at school is talking about Camden Red vs Camden Blue.' I think about his question. I feel calm. I feel cool. I feel prepared.

'Yes, I guess I do,' I reply, thinking about my Best Out of Ten kicking game with Matt. If I focus on something, I can achieve anything. The hard part is getting the team to believe the same thing. 'We need one more reserve,' I say to Alex. 'You sure you can't play?' It looks like he's not listening because he's concentrating on balancing the ball on his head.

'You know what my mum says about rugby league,' he replies, still concentrating on the ball. 'She reckons it's too rough.'

I'm about to ask him to see if his mum might change her mind, but a photocopied poster catches my attention. It's stuck on the inside of the school library's glass door, facing outwards.

'Teddy?' says Alex. He's walked ahead and hasn't realised that I'm staring at the piece of paper sticky-taped to the glass. I can't believe what I'm seeing. The top of the poster says CAMDEN BLUE IS DEAD. Someone has typed it in a font that looks like blood is dripping from the letters. Underneath the title is a picture. There are four flesh-eating zombies that someone has cut and pasted from Google Images. They've removed the original zombie faces and photoshopped Luke, Ben, Gerard and me on them instead. Also, they have somehow shaded our eyes yellow, coloured our teeth green and put blood around our mouths. Underneath the picture it says, LOVE FROM CAMDEN RED.

'Krispen and Mohamed,' I say under my

CAMDEN BLUE IS DEAD

breath. 'They're already trying to psych us out.'

'Not cool,' says Alex. We hear laughter across the walkway and see a group of boys crowding around a tree near the canteen. When we walk over, we see them looking at another copy of the zombie poster pinned to the tree trunk. One of the boys notices me standing behind them.

'Run, it's one of the

ZOMBIES!'

he shouts. They all run off, laughing. When I scan the rest of the playground, I can see that the posters are stuck to every surface imaginable. Rubbish bins, walls, stairwells, fire extinguishers and even the janitor's ride-on mower are all plastered in CAMDEN BLUE IS DEAD posters. Our faces are everywhere!

Gerard finds us next to the tree, still in shock.

'Seen this?' he says angrily, shoving a scrunched-up zombie poster in my face.

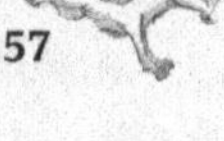

'They're all over the bus stop!'

'And all over the school – look,' I say. Gerard's face goes from angry to furious.

'Krispen and Mohamed! And that dirty Camden Red! I'm going to –'

'You're not going to do anything,' I say, cutting him off. 'We're going to let our game do the talking for us tonight.'

'But they turned us into **zombies!**' he says.

'Yeah, but you look better as a zombie than you do in real life,' I say, trying to make him laugh. Finally, he cracks a small smile. 'How about we start pulling them down?' I suggest. 'But don't throw them out – I have a plan for them,' I add.

Our last subject of the day is Design and Technology. I'm so pumped about tonight's game, I can hardly concentrate.

'Hey, boys,' says Miss Warren. 'Did you bring the 3D printer back today?'

Lewis shoots me a nervous glance.

He handed in the printed Stealth-Stud soles the other day as our finished assignment, but we haven't told Miss Warren about Damir stealing the printer yet.

'Um, it's still at my uncle's house, Miss,' he says.

'Well, I need it back on Monday please, Lewis,' she replies. Luckily Miss Warren doesn't notice that anything's wrong and she goes back to teaching the class.

Lewis looks at me and I shrug my shoulders. I know that we'll have to come clean and tell her the truth soon, but just not today – there's too much to focus on already.

'You still good for tonight?' I whisper to Lewis.

'Yeah,' he says. 'Mum, Dad, Uncle, Aunty and my cousins are even coming to watch.'

'Just remember that you're a pendulum,' I tell him. 'You can take any hit.'

'Pendulum – got it.' He smiles.

The bell rings for home time and my brain

goes into game mode. I high-five Alex, Luke, Ben and Gerard. Krispen and Mohamed are waiting at the gate for me. 'Grrrrr, zombie alert!' Krispen laughs as I walk past.

'See you tonight, Krispy Kreme,' I say, without looking up. He hates it when we call him that.

Instead of Mum picking me up, Dad is waiting for me in the ute. The radio is cranked up high and I can hear his golden oldies songs from the front gate. He taps his fingers on the steering wheel and then pretends to play the drums when the beat kicks in.

'Hey, Dad,' I say, opening the passenger-side door. He gets a fright and puts his pretend drumsticks in the pocket of his tracksuit jacket.

'Look in the back,' he says excitedly, and points. I walk around to the tray of the ute. There's a huge cardboard box there with my name and address on it, as well as a large red sticker that says, EXPRESS DELIVERY.

'What is it, Dad?' I ask. 'Can I open it now?'

'Later, mate,' he replies. 'Let's get to the fields – we've got some prep to do,' and, after I hop in, he accelerates quickly out of the pick-up zone. In the footwell is a paper bag full of afternoon tea for me, and a cold orange juice is sitting in the cup holder. I can tell that Dad's had a nap today, because

he is buzzing and full of energy. 'How'd you go at school? Did you get us one more player?' he asks. Dad knows he can ask this now because Mum's not in the car. Also, he knows that I won't get upset.

'Not yet,' I say.

'Not yet?' he repeats. 'James, we only have two hours until kick-off.'

'Don't worry, Dad,' I tell him reassuringly. 'I have a feeling he will come.'

Teddy's Tips No. 15

Everyone is equal

Treat people the way you'd like to be treated on and off the field. We are all unique and we all have something to teach each other.

CHAPTER 16

THE PERFECT BOOT

The large cardboard box in the back of Dad's ute is teasing me as it sits unopened while I do the usual jobs of getting the drink bottles ready, inflating the warm-up balls and stocking the first-aid kit. I'm imagining the game against Camden Red over and over in my head, visualising the things that I'll be doing in an hour's time. Kicking, passing, finding space, guiding my team and targeting Camden Red's weak spots are just a few of the things I'm preparing for.

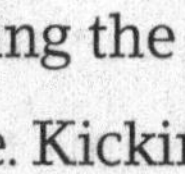

The first players to arrive are Michael and Mikayla. Michael's cracking jokes and mucking around, but Mikayla is in the zone, which is exactly where I want her to be. Next up are Gerard, Luke and Ben. They're holding a bagful of the zombie posters that were displayed around the school today.

'Got the sticky tape?' I say, raising my eyebrows.

'Right here,' says Gerard, patting his pocket.

'You know what to do,' I tell him. Gerard and the other two walk into our change room and begin their work. Tobias, Patty and Tawera rock up, followed by Dexter and Connor.

While the rest of our team is arriving, so is Camden Red. They're all decked out in brand new red, white and blue Camden Rams tracksuits. They look a million bucks.

'Hey!' calls Tawera, getting the attention of their captain and halfback Shawn Sharpe. A few of their other players turn around as well.

'Where did you get the flash gear from?' Tawera asks them. 'How come we don't get tracksuits, Coach?' he asks, turning to Dad, but Shawn gets in first.

'They only give the good stuff to the A teams, not the B teams, dummy!' He laughs and so does the rest of his team.

'Yeah, well, A stands for average and B stands for best!' Tawera calls out after them, but Shawn and the rest of Camden Red have already disappeared into their dressing shed. Soli and Amiri arrive carrying a bucket of chicken drumsticks and munch on them as they approach the change room. Dad suggests that they put it away and save it for after the game, so they don't get a stitch. Last but not least is Lewis, looking excited to be playing his first game of footy.

'Take these, Lewis,' says Lewis's mum, handing him a box of bandaids.

'This too,' instructs his dad, shoving some

headgear on Lewis's head and strapping it tightly underneath his chin. Dad takes Lewis's mum and dad aside and explains that he'll be safe and that he'll be eased gently into the game. Suddenly, I remember the unopened parcel in Dad's ute.

'Lewis, come and give me a hand,' I say. I climb up into the back of the ute and go to slide the large, heavy box down to the

tailgate, but Lewis has already reached over the side and lifted it above his head.

'Where should we put it?' he asks.

'In here,' I say, and he follows me into the change rooms where everyone is getting ready. Lewis places the box gently on the floor.

'You going to open that or what?' Tawera says from his seat in front of his locker.

I take some scissors from the first-aid kit, slice the sticky tape down the middle of the lid and pop the sides up. I try and see inside, but it's too dark. Everyone else is craning their necks to get a glimpse of the contents.

'Open it all the way!' says Ben again, impatiently. So I do. I slide the scissors down the length of the box until the sides collapse and the insides explode outwards. When the team react to what's inside, it's like a hundred golden bars have fallen out of it. And in a way, they kind of have.

'Did you know about this?' I gasp, looking at Lewis. 'Did you do this?'

'No, Teddy, not me! But I think I know who did,' he says.

'Who?'

'Miss Warren. She's the only one I gave the Stealth-Stud soles to,' he says.

In front of us is a pile of orange shoeboxes with Nike footy boots inside. On each shoebox there's the Nike tick and the word 'Stealth Studs' in the corner. There's an envelope sticking out from underneath the fallen boxes. I reach down and open it.

'Read it to us, read it to us!' pleads Tawera. So I do.

Dear Lewis and James,

Congratulations on a wonderful assignment. I am very impressed by your abilities to design and create something so useful.

I hope you don't mind, but I passed your 3D printouts of the Stealth-Stud sole to a friend at Nike. They have turned them into the perfect boot.

Hopefully there are enough boots for your whole team in this parcel.

Now go and kick Camden Red's butt!

From your teacher,
Miss Warren

PS: I need the 3D printer back ASAP please.

'No way!' I say, refolding the letter and placing it back into the envelope. The rest of the team can't believe it either. They're just sitting there in awe of the bright blue boots with the orange soles and yellow Nike tick. Camden Red might have flash new tracksuits, but I bet they don't have a footy boot sponsor!

Teddy's Tips No. 16

We all make mistakes

Behind every mistake is a lesson. Take the time to reflect and grow from your experiences.

CHAPTER 17

WHO ARE WE?

We have just put our new boots on. Usually Dad would be launching into his pre-game presentation by now, but he's not here. In fact, no one knows where he is. He better get here soon or I'll be giving the team instructions instead. There's a knock on the door. It's the referee. 'Five minutes until kick-off,' he says.

I nod and look behind the referee for any sign of Dad, but he's nowhere to be found.

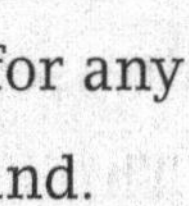

Just then I hear music start up outside the dressing room but it's not coming from the footy field's PA system – it sounds like it's being played through a cheap set of speakers. Suddenly I recognise the song. It's 'Thriller' by Michael Jackson, one of Mum's favourites. The bassline from the start of the song gets louder as the speakers get closer to the dressing room. I recognise the voices of the ladies working at the canteen screaming with laughter. Whoever is out there must be having fun. The bassline continues, *bah-doo-doo-doo-dum, bah-doo-doo-doo-dum*. It's really rocking now, and it begins to echo down the hallway of the dressing shed.

Suddenly Mikayla lets out a shriek as she spots someone coming into the dressing room. Then Patty screams! Then Tawera! The opening lyrics of the song bounce off the tiled floor as Dad struts into the room dressed as a zombie from Michael Jackson's 'Thriller' film clip. He's wearing an old ripped tracksuit, yellow horror-movie false teeth and has white makeup all over his face and black rings around his eyes. He holds his arms out in front of him like the walking dead, and in one hand he has an old Bluetooth speaker from the tractor shed.

A few of us start to laugh when we realise what we're seeing. Dad puts the speaker on the floor and claps his hands over his head, encouraging us to do the same, so we do. Now that our team is clapping the beat, Dad does the Michael Jackson moonwalk across the tiles in his gumboots and everyone cheers, 'WOOHOO!' From the speaker the bassline continues to roll on, *bah-doo-doo-doo-dum, bah-doo-doo-doo-dum.*

Then Dad does something I've never seen him do. He drops down with his legs wide apart and does the full splits! Then he springs back up like a pair of scissors snipping together and keeps dancing!

CAMDEN BLUE GOES NUTS!

Dad then runs zombie-style over to the wall and begins ripping down one of the zombie posters that Luke, Gerard and Ben stuck up earlier. Again, everyone cheers, knowing that Shawn and his mates were the ones who created them. Zombie-Dad waves everyone in the team over to do the same. In less than five seconds, the whole team is ripping down the zombie posters and singing along to the song at the same time. When all the posters are gone, Dad throws the

Bluetooth speaker to Mikayla and motions us to follow him like a team of zombies, so we do. The Camden Blue zombies stagger down the hallway with their arms outstretched, Dad and Mikayla leading the way. We lurch and stumble outside like the zombies from the film clip. Then Dad turns the corner and marches straight into the dressing shed of Camden Red.

'What's that noise?' I hear Coach Sharpe ask as we approach. Coach Sharpe's question is soon answered when the Camden Blue zombie flash mob takes over their dressing shed and Dad starts doing the moonwalk again in front of Camden Red. They have no idea what's going on! Shawn backs away into the wall and Krispen sits down next to his kit bag and cuddles his towel.

Dad pulls one of the crumpled zombie posters out of his tracksuit pants pocket and holds it up. Mikayla can see that he's about to speak, so she cuts the music. Everyone falls silent.

'Camden Red don't respect you!' Dad says to us before remembering his zombie teeth are still in. He pops his fingers into his mouth and pulls out the horror fangs. 'Look at these posters they've made – they think tonight's game is a joke!' he continues. Coach Sharpe goes to say something, but Dad waves him away. 'Are you actually okay with this, Camden Blue?' Dad asks, pointing at the poster again. 'Well?'

'Not me!' yells Mikayla. She looks around for support.

'Not me either!' I say, standing with her. Gerard soon follows me and drapes his arm over my shoulder. Ben follows him and does the same. Soon enough, the whole team is shoulder to shoulder in a circle around Zombie-Dad inside the Camden Red dressing room.

'WHO ARE WE?' Dad screams.

'BLUE!' we scream back.

'WHO ARE WE?' he repeats.

'BLUE!' we scream again.

'WHO?'

'BLUE!'

'WHO?'

'BLUE! BLUE! BLUE! BLUE! BLUE! BLUE! BLUE! BLUE! BLUE! BLUE! BLUE! BLUE!'

'NOW GO AND SHOW EVERYONE WHO WE ARE!' Dad bellows, pointing at the doorway. The screaming army of Camden Blue zombies run out of the dressing shed and onto the field, ready for the game of our lives.

We win the toss and Camden Red will kick to us. Even though it's technically a home game for us, with two Camden teams playing, the crowd is split. Mum, Nonna, Nonno and Matt are up in the stands, all wearing blue.

Nonno has his New South Wales State of Origin beanie on and his binoculars stuck to his face, watching the action. He is looking right at Shawn placing the kicking tee on the halfway line and balancing the ball on it. Camden Red form a line on either side of him and prepare for the kick downfield. The referee blows his whistle and WHACK! The ball travels deep into our half. It's a white speck in the night sky, but it comes zooming back to earth quickly and straight towards me. I snap into action, judge the landing zone and run towards it. The ball drops perfectly into my arms and I cradle it on my chest before taking the first run of the game.

'Settle it, Teddy!' yells Luke across

the field. He's right, I need to take control and build some momentum without taking too many risks. Their defence comes racing towards me, but I can already tell they're moving too quickly. I zoom past their winger and step their centre, who has already left the formation of their defensive line. Krispen lunges at me to make the game's first tackle, but I wriggle from his grip. I've already made an easy 20 metres. I spot a small opportunity in the middle of the field and run inwards to draw the rest of the defenders. Just a few more seconds and I can put Tobias into a gap – BOOM! Shawn appears from nowhere and catches me off guard. He drives me into the ground. It feels like I've been hit by a truck. I take a breath and get straight to my feet – I can't let Shawn know I'm rattled.

'Amiri! First run!' yells Ben.

Amiri steams onto the ball and collides with Camden Red's solid wall of defence.

OOOOF!

Three tacklers hang off Amiri and suddenly the ball comes loose.

'Dive on it!' yells Mohamed from Camden Red. Amiri is protesting to the ref that the ball has been raked out of his hands. Instead of diving on it and taking the tackle, Camden Red's centre scoops the ball and begins to run in open space. Michael is chasing him, but he's too far behind.

'All the way!' shouts Shawn to his player, who is sprinting to the tryline. Michael has made some ground but it's not enough. Their centre dives over the line and scores under the posts.

'Nice hands, big fella!' says Shawn sarcastically to Amiri, and pats him on the back. Amiri hangs his head, knowing he's let us down. 'Get used to those points going up there,' Shawn teases me, pointing at the scoreboard. He laughs and runs over to kick the conversion. We're six points down after two minutes.

Not the start we wanted at all.

Teddy's Tips No. 17

Thank you

Before a match, I would always show gratitude towards my parents, coach and teammates. Every night write down three things you are grateful for from that day.

CHAPTER 18

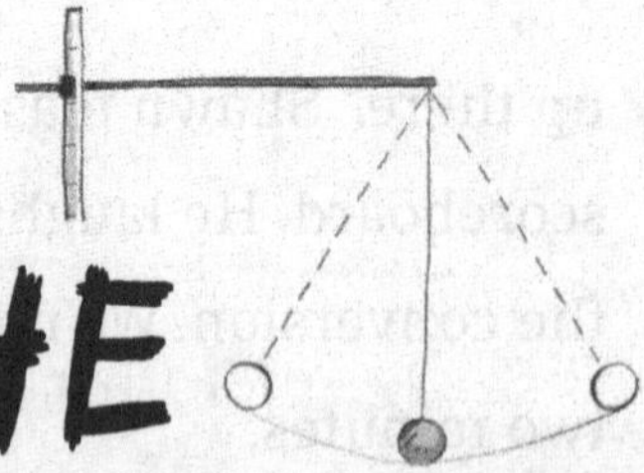

BE THE PENDULUM

They scored, so we kick to them. As soon as they receive the ball, I see what their game plan is. It's pretty simple – run at Mikayla. Her eyes are like dinner plates as she sees the runners getting ready.

'Get over and help her!' I scream at the team. Mikayla is brave and takes down the first runner in a courageous tackle, but the onslaught is relentless. Runner after runner targets the weak line of defence on Mikayla's wing. Soon enough, it's the fifth tackle and Shawn chips a tricky little ball angled infield. I race to defuse the play but the ball bounces awkwardly and straight back into Shawn's hands. He scores by placing the ball on the grass and celebrates his try by picking it back up and throwing it over the dead ball line like a hand grenade.

'That's my boy!' yells Coach Sharpe from the sideline. 'Too easy!' He laughs. My blood is boiling. First it was the zombie posters and now it's the disrespect on display by Camden Red *and* their coach.

'You can kick this with your eyes closed!' yells Dakota from Camden Red. Shawn doesn't close his eyes, but he kicks the conversion easily. In under ten minutes the score has gone to 0–12.

On his way back to the halfway mark, Shawn smiles at me and points at the scoreboard again.

With five minutes to go until halftime,

the score has ballooned out to 0–18. If that isn't bad enough, two more bad things happen. Very bad things.

'ARRGGGH!'

screams Soli after making a tackle. The referee immediately stops play and Dad runs out to Soli. The rest of the team stand back while I join Dad and Soli, who's writhing in pain.

'My ankle! I think it's broken!' he sobs. Dad pulls down Soli's sock carefully. Soli winces when Dad touches him.

'Hmmm, don't know if it's broken, but you've definitely rolled it,' Dad says, studying Soli. 'We'd better get you off the field.' Soli shakes his head.

'No, Coach – we've only got one reserve,' he says through gritted teeth.

'You're right,' says Dad. 'And we're going to use him.' Dad turns to the referee. 'He's coming off, we'll bring out our only reserve.'

Dad helps Soli to his feet and supports him as he hobbles off the field. Out comes Lewis, taking deep breaths.

'Be the pendulum, be the pendulum,' he's saying to himself. Unfortunately, Lewis doesn't get the chance to put his scientific knowledge to the test before halftime. In the next play, the second very bad thing happens. Camden Red's fullback intercepts a sloppy pass from Tawera and runs 30 metres to score in the corner. They miss the conversion but then the halftime siren sounds and it's 0–22. There's no way back from here.

The dressing shed is stone cold silent as we come in for our five-minute break. The only sounds are of us sipping from our water bottles and our forwards sucking in oxygen after having to run more than usual. I try to find the words needed to motivate the team, but I'm numb. I didn't think the game would go this way. The squelch of Dad's gumboots can be heard on the tiles again as he enters the shed.

'You want to know how I'm feeling?' he finally says after walking around in a circle, making eye contact with everyone at least once. 'I'm disappointed, that's how I feel.' No one says anything. The mood has changed from before. No music, no clapping, but Dad still has the black rings painted around his eyes. We're all disappointed with ourselves. We can play better footy than this. 'In fact, I'm also feeling tired. I'm tired of talking,' he says. He puts his clipboard under his arm and starts walking out the door.

'Dad! Don't go!' I say. 'Let's talk about what we need to do!' Very quickly, in what feels like a millisecond, Dad gives me a

WINK.

Instantly I know that he's letting me in on a joke. He always winks at Matt and me when he's about to play a trick on Mum. It's his way of saying, 'Just play along with me on this.' Lucky for me, I know what Dad is trying to do.

'No, James, I already told you, I'm sick of talking. Remember, actions speak louder than words!' He pulls a mobile phone out of the pocket of his ripped tracksuit jacket and, to everyone's astonishment, throws it into the bucket of iced water used to fill the drink bottles. It splashes the players sitting next to the bucket and sinks to the bottom like an anchor being thrown from a fishing boat. The whole team gasps in disbelief. They look at the phone and then at him, but Dad walks past us, throwing me another quick little wink before marching out the door. Most of the players are murmuring to each other in shock, their eyes still glued to Dad's waterlogged phone.

'Okay, guys,' I say, getting up and standing in Dad's place. I know Dad's trying to help, and I won't let him down. It was like his wink gave me a blast of energy. 'Let's face it,

it's going to be impossible to win from here, but we can at least show Coach that we're prepared to put up a fight!'

'That's right,' says Mikayla. 'We owe it to Coach to start stepping up.'

Players start to nod their heads in agreement.

'Remember, Soli's injured, so we don't have any reserves,' I remind them. 'We need to look out for each other!' By now the team are standing and rallying around.

I'm about to walk the team back out when there's a sudden knock at the door.

'Actually, you've got one more reserve,' says a familiar voice. It's Alex, who has just finished his game of club soccer and still has his boots on.

'Mum said it's okay for me to play an extra sport. Rugby league it is!' Alex smiles. 'I guess I won't need these.' He laughs, sliding the shin protectors out from his socks.

A wave of energy comes over the team

as they see Alex in the doorway, shining like an Italian soccer god. Luke, Ben and Gerard get off their seats and wrap their arms around him.

'He's a Ram!' says Ben.

'A *blue* Ram, not a red one!' Luke laughs. I throw Alex a spare jersey.

'What position do want me in?' he asks.

'It doesn't matter,' I say. 'Let's just have some fun.'

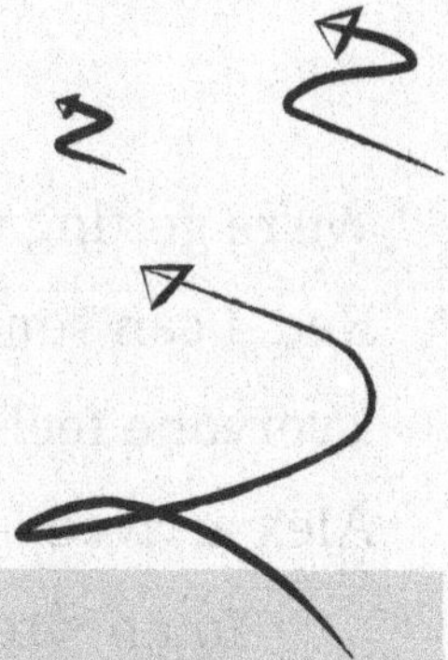

Teddy's Tips No. 18

Listen to your body

It's important to always rest and recover after a game. If you don't get enough rest, then you won't get the best out of your body.

CHAPTER 19

ACTIONS SPEAK LOUDER

We're getting ready to kick off to Camden Red. I can sense the shift in our team's mood. Everyone feels a bit more upbeat since Alex arrived.

'You heard the coach, actions speak louder than words!' I say.

They all nod.

'Play your part!' I shout, before running forward and kicking the ball downfield.

Camden Blue runs a solid line of

defence and I can hear our players talking, telling each other who they are marking or when they need to slide across to cover the attackers.

'Get ready, Lewis!' I say. 'You've got this runner – be the pendulum!' Mohamed, who plays second row for Camden Red, grips the ball and runs like a bull at a matador, except our matador is a 92-kilogram Samoan giant. It's clear Mohamed thinks that Lewis will be a pushover, but he's soon to discover that he's making a big mistake.

BANG!

Lewis knocks Mohamed off his feet and crash-tackles him into the dew-capped grass. Mohamed loses the ball on impact, and just like Camden Red's first try, Michael plucks the ball off the ground and goes into 100-metre sprint mode.

'Go yourself!' I yell behind him. 'You've got this!'

Michael is outrunning their fullback and flecks of soil and turf flick up from his Stealth Studs as he crosses the tryline to score under the posts. Everyone down the far end of the field mobs Lewis and congratulates him on such a powerful tackle. Michael's lungs are screaming for oxygen after his length-of-the-field try. His hands are on his knees as he gasps for air.

'Michael!' yells Dad. 'Come and have a breather!' Michael runs across to the sideline where Alex is eagerly awaiting his Camden Blue debut. 'Alex, go and make some magic!' says Dad.

Knowing that time isn't on our side, I push to take the conversion as quickly as I can. Shawn and his mates start heckling again, trying to put me off like last game. What they don't know is that my practice with Matt means I am ready to block them out this time. I kick the two points and look up at Matt in the grandstand, who is giving me the thumbs up. Six points to 22, with 18 minutes to go.

Our next try is the result of some razzle-dazzle footwork from our newest recruit, Alex. He spins and turns, dodges and steps – no one can lay their hands on him.

When he's finally caught around the legs, he offloads a quick ball to Patty, who passes to Connor who gets it to me. I run as fast as I can to the left corner of the field, their outside backs in hot pursuit. From the corner of my eye I see Mikayla in support.

If I don't pass it soon, they'll take me down and we'll lose momentum.

I take a chance and throw a long ball to Mikayla, and it lands right on her chest. She continues towards the left-hand corner. Their fullback runs across to take her down, but he overruns and she steps inside him. He tries to correct himself, but slides over awkwardly on the slippery grass. Unmarked, Mikayla loops around to score another try for Camden Blue under the posts, just like Michael did. My legs are screaming for a rest after the last play. I hand the conversion over to Gerard, who is successful. With 15 minutes to go, the score is 12–22.

Incredibly, that's only the beginning. The next two tries come about from the hard work of our forward pack. Amiri and Patty make some easy metres until Ben at hooker tells Lewis to get ready for the last run before the ball is given to the backs. Lewis takes his position and I can tell he's visualising the pendulum again.

He catches the ball that Luke pops up and moves forward like a steamroller, flattening anyone in his path. As soon as a tackler ricochets off him, they get back up and try tackling him again, only to bounce off once more.

'Go, Lewis!' screams Dad from the sideline, jumping up and down. I notice he's holding on to another phone. Weird.

Lewis has at least five players holding on to him now, but he keeps moving forward, not taking a backward step. He's moved 30 metres like this and is only 20 metres out from the tryline. In what seems an eternity for Camden Red, Lewis finally stumbles to the ground. Tawera takes advantage of a beautiful cut-out pass from Ben and scoots over to score in the corner. While Lewis is being congratulated by our team, Shawn is losing his cool with Camden Red.

'Idiots!' he screams at them. 'Just tackle him! He's not even any good!'

Gerard wants another go at the conversion.

He lines it up and . . . misses! The score is 16 points to 22. Camden Red is still in the lead.

As Camden Red kick off to us again, Luke is momentarily distracted by something on the sideline. I spot Breeanna sitting on the bench next to Dad. Beside her is Rocco, who's lying at her feet and munching happily on the grass. She waves at Luke and he smiles.

'Luke! The ball!' I scream. Just in time, Luke looks up and catches the ball before it hits him in the face. He stands there and looks back at Breeanna.

'Luke! Now run!' I say.

Luke takes it up quickly and is tackled on halfway. Ben gets it to Connor, Connor to Alex. Again, Alex's speedy footwork leaves the defence bamboozled. Without even being touched, he runs to the right corner and dives over the line. The crowd goes up.

Even Rocco lets out a

'MAAAAA.'

'Ladies and gentlemen, this is going to be a close one,' booms the ground announcer into the microphone. 'Camden Red continue to lead Camden Blue, 22 points to 20. Five minutes until fulltime!' Coach Sharpe is on the sideline, screaming out instructions to

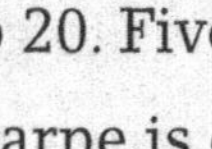

his team. He's not happy that we've scored again. This time I take the conversion. It's a pressure kick and if I get this, we'll level the score at 22 points all. I place the ball on the kicking tee, step forward, look at the posts and then step back. I step forward again and kick . . .

AND I MISS!

I could beat myself up like last time, but I know it won't help. Instead, I visualise what I need to do next, which is lead our team to victory. Camden Red jump and high-five each other. They're still in the lead.

The next few minutes are an arm wrestle. The momentum has shifted in our direction and we are letting our actions speak louder than our words. Camden Red complete a full set of six and we run the ball back, desperately trying to score again before fulltime. Two minutes to go. We're 30 metres out. The ball goes across the field to Alex, who tries to penetrate their line, but he can't. It comes back the other way, from Ben to Gerard, Gerard to Connor. Then Connor is tackled right in front of the posts. I hear him yelling. 'My foot! Where is my foot?' Connor's prosthetic foot has fallen off in the tackle and he can't stand up. Shawn sees it lying on the ground and picks it up and flicks it over the dead ball line when he thinks the referee isn't watching.

PFFFFT!

The referee blows his whistle.

'Unsportsmanlike conduct,' he says to Shawn. Ten minutes in the bin! Shawn is blowing up and so is his team. Not only has he given us a penalty right in front of the goalposts, Camden Red are now down to 12 players. Gerard runs over.

'Take the two points or go for the try?' he says. Two points will take us to a draw, but that's not why we came here tonight.

'Let's go all out!' I say. 'We're going for the try, Camden Blue!' I shout.

Connor has been given his foot back and he takes the tap 20 metres out. I don't need my Spidey senses and game of join-the-dots tonight. I can already see who our match-winning try scorer will be. Connor passes to Ben, who passes to Gerard, who then passes to me. I play with their centre, stepping him, moving forward, stepping back, slowly inching my way to Mikayla's wing. Once there's an overlap from a shortage of defenders, I pass the ball to Mikayla and she spots the opening. The rest is history. Mikayla places the ball over the line and the crowd erupts. Camden Blue comes from behind to take the lead, 24 points to 22 with the kick to come. Thirty seconds remain until fulltime –

IT'S IN THE BAG

I line up the ball. Even though we've won the game, I still want to kick this. It's a tough kick but I've kicked plenty of these before. This time there're no distractions coming from Camden Red, but there's a voice in the crowd I recognise.

'BUTT RASH!' he shouts. I kick the ball and it curves in slightly, moving perfectly between the posts. I look up at the grandstand and give Matt a smile. Camden Blue defeat Camden Red 26 points to 22.

'Dad?' I say from the back seat. Mum is fiddling with the car radio, trying to find a song she likes.

'Yes, mate?' he says, his fingers tapping away on the steering wheel to the music Mum has just found.

'Which phone did you throw in the water?' I point at his mobile phone which is sitting in the phone holder on the dash.

'Not that one,' he says, smiling.

'Which phone was it?' I ask.

'My old work phone,' he says. 'It was already broken. I accidentally ran over it with the car two years ago.' Matt takes his earphones out and starts laughing.

'Best trick ever,' he says.

'Did you know Dad was going to do that?' I asked him.

'Yep. Didn't know about the zombie stuff though.' He sticks his earphones back in.

'Well, you were playing Camden Red. I had to try every trick in the book!' Dad says, glancing at me over his shoulder before returning his gaze to the road. 'Because it's true, actions speak louder than words.'

Mum looks at Dad proudly. 'He's full of surprises, your dad,' she says with a smile.

'He sure is,' I reply.

Teddy's Tips No. 19

Be patient!

Good things take time. Stay committed and focused, and don't give up. Always give whatever you choose to do 110 per cent.

CHAPTER 20

SAY HELLO TO MY LITTLE FRIEND

If we can beat Camden Red, we can do anything, on the field and off.

After our win, Lewis and I muster the confidence to go and retrieve Miss Warren's 3D printer from Damir. We decide to try the mall first, hoping he hasn't taken it home yet. As we're walking there on Saturday morning, we spot Damir and his trolley boys in their high-vis vests going down a back alley. In a lucky break for us, they actually have the

3D printer with them. It's loaded inside a shopping trolley.

'Hey!' I yell. 'That's ours!' Damir and the others spin around to face us.

'Well, look who it is – the mad scientist and his little chihuahua!' Damir's mates laugh at his dumb joke. 'You're too late. We're going to hock this at Cash Converters.'

'No way,' says Lewis. 'You stole that from us.' Lewis is nervous but not as much as last time.

Damir holds on to the handle of the shopping trolley and shoves it towards us to see if we flinch. Unfortunately, we do. They all laugh again.

'Listen, just give us the printer and we won't talk to you ever again,' I say as calmly as I can.

Damir is losing his cool. This time he steps from behind the trolley and raises his fist, ready to punch me again. Then we hear a voice coming from the dark of the alley, behind Damir and the others.

'I wouldn't do that if I were you,' they say.

'Who – who's that?' asks Damir, trying to see into the shadows.

Luke steps out from behind a wheelie bin.

'Ha!' Damir laughs. 'It's only the little jerk who stole my girlfriend!'

Damir gets ready to punch Luke as well.

'It's not me you need to worry about,' says Luke.

Damir suddenly looks uncertain. 'Who else is in there with you?' he sneers, peering into the shadows again.

'Say hello to my little friend!' says Luke.

Rocco springs from behind the wheelie bin on a dog leash like a Rottweiler. Luke releases him from the lead and Rocco charges straight at Damir.

'MAAAA,' bleats Rocco, running full pelt at Damir. He's dipping his head low and showing his impressive horns as his hooves clip-clop on the concrete pavement at speed.

'RUN!' screams Damir. He and his mates run like lightning back down the alleyway with Rocco in hot pursuit. Lewis, Luke and I are crying with laughter at the sight of Breeanna's billygoat chasing down the so-called tough trolley boys.

I take the trolley with the 3D printer and wheel it slowly back towards the mall. Lewis walks with me and Luke sits on the front, getting a free ride. 'You know what this calls for?' asks Luke.

'No idea,' says Lewis.

'A celebration?' I say.

'You got it, Teddy!' Luke laughs.

'Milkshakes?' I ask.

'No, even better than milkshakes,' says Luke. 'Want to know what's better than milkshakes?' he adds.

'What?' asks Lewis.

'Cheese,' Luke replies. 'Let's go get some cheese.'

Teddy's Tips No. 20

Lean into things

Life goes on. Don't hold on to things that you can't control. Learn the lesson and move on.

THE END

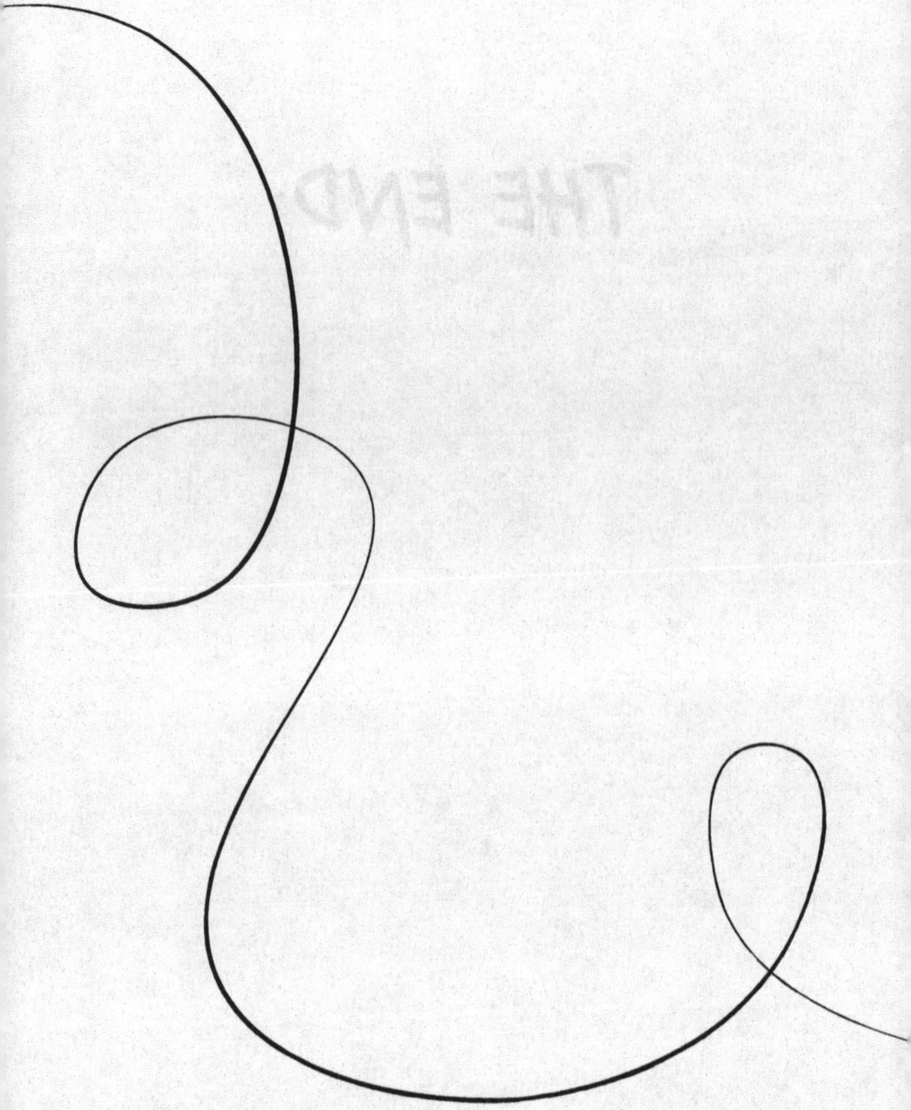

COLNELL

CONELL
LANDSCAPING
4636 6084

JAMES TEDESCO
HAT-TRICK TEDDY
ILLUSTRATED BY
HEATH McKENZIE
OUT NOW